HER FORTUNE WAS THE PRICE
ON HER HEAD!

Burt Keating had been trying to make the acquaintance of his pretty red-headed neighbor but he wasn't getting very far until the day she escaped from a strange roadside encounter. For when it turned out that murder had resulted from the affair, she threw herself hysterically into Burt's arms, pleading for his help.

It seems she had inherited a sealed box, whose contents were entirely unknown. Certain parties wanted that box badly. They had offered her a fortune—or sudden death.

Burt knew then that chivalry can go too far, for there was no longer any way out once he'd tangled with THE QUAKING WIDOW.

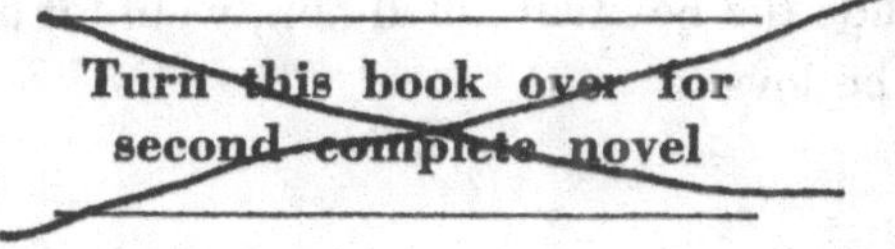

Turn this book over for second complete novel

CAST OF CHARACTERS

ALICIA SHAFTON

Her widow's legacy paid off in MURDER!

BURT KEATING

He tried to lose a memory—he almost lost his life.

JACK CANNOVA

Shoemaking was his hobby—only the shoes were filled with lead.

MILLICENT EMORY

She excelled in the three M's—Men, Money and MURDER.

RALPH EMORY

He bought the mysterious box—but it turned out to be a coffin.

GEORGE McCABE

He made the box that killed him; would it also kill the woman he loved?

The Quaking Widow

Robert Colby

PROLOGUE BOOKS

F+W Media, Inc.

Published in electronic format by
PROLOGUE BOOKS
an imprint of F+W Media, Inc.
10151 Carver Road
Blue Ash, Ohio 45242
www.prologuebooks.com

eISBN 10: 1-4405-3687-2
eISBN 13: 978-1-4405-3687-8
POD ISBN 10: 1-4405-5516-8
POD ISBN 13: 978-1-4405-5516-9

This work has been previously published in print format by:
Ace Books, Inc.

CHAPTER ONE

A MAN can get into a lot of trouble if he's lonely. If he's just lonely enough and has time on his hands. That's a combination made for trouble. And if he's lonely, has time and also a little money—you've got to have money or you're busy fretting about it—there are no end of possibilities. I had all three—loneliness, time and a certain amount of money. And my loneliness was not an ordinary loneliness. It was at first morbid and then bitter. It was during the bitter time, the self-pitying time, that I met Alicia Shafton under such strange circumstances, it seemed inevitable that what followed was stranger still.

I lived with my wife, Beverly, in a small town not far from Buffalo, New York. We had a small, comfortable home which had been left to my wife when her grandmother died. It had the rare advantage of being paid for. Bev was twenty-eight, and, at thirty-six, I was the manager of a small branch loan company in Buffalo, a job I had ascended to in the course of time and events. It was no more than a decent income, but we saved and prospered. We had no children.

We were certainly happy, even though we never stopped to think about it. It wasn't that kind of happiness. It wasn't wild or ecstatic, just comfortable and secure, immensely companionable and familiar, full of needs met in quiet understanding. It was a small fire of love, but deeply banked.

Bev was not one to turn your head about on the street, or to startle you at her entrance into a room. She was small and dark-haired with a trim little figure, a shy smile and an unobtrusive manner. You warmed to her slowly and had to search her out. But if you took the trouble to dig under the placid surface, you found a rich vein of trust and courage and understanding. Also a wry good humor. Suffice to say, she didn't set me on fire, she slowly engulfed me with the need for her, and after we were married, I never thought of being without her. It was unthinkable.

And then one night I came home in the early darkness of winter, tired from the weary drive over icy roads in endless streams of snarled and cautious traffic, put the car in the garage, glad it was over, and lay on the big double bed reading the paper while Bev rustled in the kitchen.

"Did you put the car away, honey?" she called.

"Unh-huh," I muttered absently.

She came into the room, a still, small presence. "We're all out of butter," she said. "And I need flour. Wouldn't you know!"

"I'll go," I said wearily, not wanting to.

There was a pause. "You look so comfortable. It'll only take me a minute."

"Well . . ." I said, dropping the paper a moment, "if you really . . ."

She patted my head. "Where are the keys?"

"In my overcoat pocket."

She left the room. In a moment I heard the front door close quietly, the distant murmur of the car being backed out. It was one of those times I was a little thoughtless, letting her baby my tiredness. Again I became absorbed with the paper. Her little errand, the bitter night, left my thoughts. Strangely, it was one of the few times I had not called something to her like,

"Hurry home," or "Miss you, baby," or just "So long, honey."

She never came back. It happened just a few blocks away. A car came out of a cross street fast and skidding out of control on the ice, a big Buick, crushing our little car against a tree—and frail little Beverly inside.

I sold the house. And there was an insurance settlement and savings. But a million dollars wouldn't have touched me where I hurt. I went through the job like a robot, that part of me that could look at the truth for more than an awful moment, paralyzed, locked away. In the end they had to give me an indefinite leave of absence. That was when I went to Florida and moved like a zombie through the lush days and nights until I met Alicia Shafton.

I bought a new car, an Olds Convertible, and headed South. I wanted to flee to a new world and I knew that short of some South Pacific island, southern Florida was as close as you could come. After a few restless days in Miami, I took an apartment on the beach at Ft. Lauderdale some twenty miles away. It was a place called the Tropic Moon Apartments.

It was a long, rambling structure, low in spite of its three stories, U-shaped and the largest apartment building I could find fronting the ocean. It must have contained some forty or fifty units, which was fine because I wanted to be swallowed up and anonymous.

It was living on a very grand and expensive scale. The building wasn't over a year old, extremely modern, the apartments lavishly furnished with picture windows that overlooked the sea, each having a small, private patio. The wide, deep lawn was decked with tall, well groomed palm trees, tropic vegetation and an assortment of colorful flowers. Scattered about were those round metal tables, from the centers of which sprung great gaudy umbrellas.

For the first week or ten days I talked to no one. I

cooked my own breakfast, spent longer and longer hours on the beach as my skin became adjusted to the sun, had a lonely dinner and a drink at a nearby hotel, then read myself into oblivion and started over again.

That was the morbid time, that first week, and I was so full of my loss there was no room for even the thought of anyone or anything in the future.

Then gradually, I don't know when it began exactly, there was a subtle change in my attitude. The sorrow became tinged with resentment, then pure hatred that I lived in a world where, in the space of minutes from the time Beverly left me snug and secure in the certainty of limitless time shared together, some blind crazy force could take her away, voiding her life, actually, and mine, figuratively, at the same moment. I was terribly sorry for Bev, yes, but since I still lived, even sorrier for myself. Much of the warmth I had had for life and humanity left me. Melancholy was replaced with bitterness and I became determined to wreak a kind of revenge. But on who? On what? There was nothing to strike at—except, perhaps, life itself.

It was then that I became aware of Alicia. I say aware because actually I had seen her on the second day of my arrival at the Tropic Moon Aprtment, but had only marked her subconsciously. I did not see her again until the second week of my stay, which in itself was curious because she was a type I would have noticed in any state of mind. That first time, I passed her in the breezeway to her remote, third-floor apartment. I watched the door close behind her and though she was but three doors from my own, I never saw her leave or enter again for over a week. Nor did I see her anywhere about the building or on the beach. And on this day, when I saw her again, it was her absence rather than her presence, which seemed most strange.

This time she was coming out of her apartment. I couldn't be sure, but I had the feeling that she was alone, that she hadn't left the apartment since the last time I saw her, that she was watchful of something or somebody—and afraid. I was sure of one thing. She was the most beautiful woman I had ever seen. And as she came toward me down the breezeway with her soundless, careful step, I was suddenly curious. If for no other reason than to occupy myself with a fresh current of thought, I decided to find out about her.

She was medium tall. Her hair was auburn and long. Her face was more round than oval. The first thing you saw, when you could take your eyes off her figure, was her mouth. It was a wide splash across her face with a full-blown cushion of lower lip. A prominent mouth that still managed to look sensitive and without vulgarity. The cheek bones were high and softly rounded, the nose small and upturned with a flare of nostrils, like a fine animal sensing a crisp autumn day. It was a face that argued intelligence and refinement against sensuality, a combination I found intriguing. She was not just a doll. She was a mentality. And from the look of her chin, something to cope with.

She came toward me in the soft-stepping manner of one who passes through a bedroom where someone is asleep, her white, crested sweater softly ballooned with the thrust of her breasts, the white sharkskin skirt tracing the slender hipline and flow of thighs to long taper of stockinged legs. She wore little make-up and her features bore no sign of having been exposed to the sun. Strange.

I was leaning over the rail of the breezeway, watching the morning sun glint from the chrome grill of a pale green Cadillac convertible parked in front of the building. As she came abreast of me, I turned.

"Good morning," I said. "Another beautiful day."

I had the feeling she had been going to sneak by me. If I hadn't seen her, I doubt if I'd have heard her. She seemed to walk on the balls of her high-heeled shoes.

She turned her head slowly, warily. Her face was without expression. The way she stared at me, it might have been a whistle I offered her. She seemed about to move on without a word. There was the quick rotation of thought stirring behind amber-flecked, turquoise eyes. I had time to figure her in her late twenties and to be certain that she must be reasoning how odd it would be if she didn't answer such a casual remark from a fellow tenant.

"Yes," she said quietly and without a smile, "a very nice day." And then I was looking at the graceful movement of her marvelous back—going away.

The idea of discovering more about her had come to me impulsively as she left her apartment and I was without a plan. But I was positive I wouldn't get another chance. I hurried after her. "Excuse me," I said. "But do you happen to have a car here at the beach?"

Again she turned and gave me the same blank look. But her eyes betrayed her. They flicked to the green Cadillac. "Your car?" I asked.

She gave me the merest nod.

"I'm in a silly jam," I hurried on. "I have a car of my own, but this morning I discovered I'm out of gas. I wonder if I could trouble you to give me a lift to the nearest gas station? They could give me a couple of gallons and then . . ." It was the only thing I could think of. It was foolish because I was really in no mood to play games. On the other hand, there was something frantic inside me that demanded action—some kind of intrigue that would free me from thinking, thinking. And this girl was so unlike Bev, she and the Florida setting, so unlike the past.

The amber-flecked eyes looked trapped. I rushed into the silence. "Excuse me again. My name is Burt Keating. I think we live just a few doors from each other."

"How do you do," she said coldly without offering her own name. "I wish I had time to chat with you but

I'm on my way to . . . I'm in quite a hurry." It was a smoothly modulated voice containing overtones of annoyance. She was taking keys from her purse and walking briskly away. For the first time her heels struck sharply on the terrazzo floor.

I fell in beside her. "I won't even take you out of your way," I said. "You can just drop me off at the nearest gas station on your route and I'll get the attendant to drive me back."

Her silence was at least not a point blank refusal. I walked with her to the sleek, new convertible, noticing the Florida plates. When she slid behind the wheel, I climbed in beside her. The Cadillac was parked in a space diagonal to the curb, surrounded by others. She backed out easily and we purred away along the beach road. I sat back against the red leather seat and relaxed. It was somewhat out of character for me to be so aggressive, but I liked being out of character and, for the first time, I was beginning to enjoy myself. At least the dreary pattern of thought and inaction was changing.

"I see by your plates that you're a native."

"Yes . . . Well . . . uh, no. I bought the car here."

She sounded distracted. Far removed. The long, sandy beach with its people at winter play, the pale green, bathtub-warm ocean, dotted with costly yachts and fishing boats, the expensive white faces of the tourist traps, glared in the sun and slid by. And for the first time, I didn't think of Bev or myself.

"Then you're a tourist like myself."

"In a way."

"I come from around Buffalo. It's like going from the deep freeze into the fiery furnace." I thought a little information might disarm her. "I manage a loan company branch—Inter-State Loan. But I'm on an indefinite leave of absence." And when she didn't say anything still, I put myself to the test. "You see, I . . . I lost my wife in . . . in . . ." I swallowed. "In an accident. I'm in the process of trying to forget a little—if you ever can." I told her this not because of any communal feeling (she was nothing but a curiosity to me then), but because I wanted to try my wings. It was the first time I had been able to speak of Bev at all since the funeral. I felt it would be a sort of return to normalcy.

She turned and looked at me for the first time as a person. "Oh," she said. "I'm sorry." It was the first human sound that had come out of her. "Why do you tell *me*?"

"Well," I said, "I suppose I just wanted to see if I could tell *anyone*. As a matter of fact, I haven't spoken a word to anyone except our host since I've been here. About ten days. In a way, you can keep a thing from being real until you say it."

"I see. Well, I'm sorry."

"It doesn't matter. Nobody can be sorry enough—except me. What's your name?"

She looked at me again, a quick appraisal before she returned her eyes to the road. "Alicia," she said. "Alicia Shafton."

"Shafton your married name?"

"I think there's a gas station down this block," she parried. There was. She stopped in front of it. I got out. "Thank you, Alicia. See you again, I hope."

She turned that blank, far away look on me and without a word she was gone.

As soon as she was out of sight I began to walk. I walked all the way back. And enjoyed it. I didn't think of anything. I watched the surf and the swimmers, listened to the rustle of palm fronds and let the sun work at drying up the soggy self-pity and bitterness I carried always with me.

Later I waited in my apartment and watched from my window for her return. I had an idea she wouldn't come back empty-handed. You didn't hole up in an apartment for days at a time without food. And I was right. She came back loaded with groceries.

I just *happened* to be coming downstairs when she was struggling up with one of three stuffed boxes. I took the box from her before she could object and carried it to her apartment. She opened the door and took the box from me, laying it inside. She closed the door again and I walked down with her for the rest of it in silence. At the car she suddenly turned. "Look," she said. "You probably don't mean any harm and I'm sorry about your wife. But will you, for God's sake, just leave me alone! I don't need any help and if I need company I'll send for you."

"Don't do me any favors," I said. "If I want company I can walk out on the beach and find it any time. Now, do you want me to carry your goddam packages or don't you?" I couldn't help it. She was killing my first attempt to climb out of myself.

She looked startled but she lost very little composure. "I'm sorry," she said. "You have your problems, I have mine. I *would* like some help with the packages."

This time she actually let me in the apartment and allowed me to carry her stuff to the kitchen. It was probably one of the most expensive layouts in the building. There was a living room three times the size of my living-bedroom combined. There was a dining area and the kitchen was large and beautifully equipped. Through an open door I caught sight of a spacious bedroom. They had spared no expense with furnishings or decor and every room overlooked the sea. The place must be costing her two-fifty a week. And it didn't look like she was in any hurry to leave. Naturally, I wondered where she got that kind of money.

At the door she actually smiled. "Thanks a lot," she said. "You've been a big help."

"Listen," I said. "You probably need a change from cooking your own meals and so do I. Why don't you let me take you to dinner at the hotel across the way tonight?"

"Oh . . . I . . . I don't know." I could see she was

dying to go out and that she had decided whatever she was afraid of had nothing to do with me.

"Come on," I said. "Do you good."

She shook her head. "No," she said. "I'd like to, but I'm expecting a call. I can't leave."

"Too bad. Some other time maybe."

"No," she said. "I'm afraid not." I was about to go, when she said suddenly, "But if you want to catch pot luck with me, drop over around seven."

I was so surprised it took me a moment to get out, "At seven. I'll be here. And many thanks!"

As I turned to go, my eyes dropped to a blond end table by a massive chair near the door. On it was a handsome leather brief case. It looked empty. But it bore the initials G. M. When I looked into her face I could tell that she knew I had seen it and was wondering how you get G. M. out of Alicia Shafton.

Her face had returned to its emptiness. There was a cold, brittle challenge in her eyes. From her expression, I gathered that if she could gracefully do so, she would immediately cancel our dinner date. I didn't give her a chance. "At seven," I said and closed the door, taking with me the image of her still standing there, blank-faced and motionless.

CHAPTER TWO

BACK IN MY TINY APARTMENT, I undid the sofa-bed and propped myself up so I could look out to sea. A freighter on the distant horizon steamed toy-like along the coast, trailing puffs of smoke. Inshore two kids water-tobogganed on rubber mattresses. The lucid water lay like a jade-green carpet unfurling to the beach. It was just after noon.

I lighted a cigarette and began an article about atomic submarines. I put it down after a moment when I found I had read the same paragraph three times. Well, after all, there was really nothing very mysterious about a brief case engraved with G. M. instead of A. S. It could belong to her boss. Would she have one? She looked her own boss. Or it could belong to a friend or relative. Or G. M. could stand for her real name, Alicia Shafton a phony. But then, most women didn't carry brief cases. I gave up.

The point was that I would not have been more than mildly curious about the initials if her eyes, her whole manner, had not made such an issue of the matter. It's always interesting to note how we accuse ourselves so much more than others do—if we're hiding something. It's a rare one who can be perfectly natural in the concealment of himself. It takes a peculiar type of imagination and acting ability. People give themselves, their whole character away in the most casual conversation to an acute observer. And then there is an aura about them that tells more than words. It's a label they carry to the grave.

I marked Alicia as basically a good sort, but subject to many temptations. I imagined she could be swayed by impulses. And there was a certain willfulness about her. Willful people with unusual needs drive on to the end, reckless of consequences. They'll pay an outlandish price, and I don't necessarily mean money, for what they want. Will is the driving force of destruction. Alicia had that kind of will. There was, I sensed, this element of destruction in it. I wondered how far down the road she had traveled. There was one thing I was pretty sure of. She had traveled to a point of trouble. I was also pretty sure that I was going to travel with her. For a ways. She had something I needed. There was a startling excitement about her that made it next to impossible to mope around with morbid retrospection and introspection in her presence. And if she was reckless of consequences, so was I in my own way. At the moment I didn't care how I lived or whether I lived at all!

After awhile I took up the article again. This time I made it all the way through. I got lost in several other articles and began a novel. Then my phone rang. It was sometime after three. There was a switchboard down in the cubbyhole office of the building with an operator on duty from early morning to midnight. I had noticed that Alicia had an additional phone—a direct outside line, another clue that she was going to be around quite a while. I imagined this was she calling to cancel our dinner arrangement. It wasn't. It was long distance—Art Caldwell on the wire from Buffalo. Art is my assistant and he was in charge in my absence.

"Art! What a surprise. How did you locate me?"

"Don't you remember? You sent me a card from Ft. Lauderdale."

"So I did. I'm in kind of a fog these days."

"Sure. I can well understand that."

"What's on your mind? Have I still got a job?"

"At least you're joking. That's a sign of recovery. Nothing on my mind. Just called to see how you were getting along."

"Only fair, Art. Just fair. I don't need to go into details."

"Not a word."

"Any problems at the office?"

"Always. Nothing I can't handle. That's something you shouldn't be thinking about."

"Believe me, I'm not. Just making talk."

"As a matter of fact, Burt, someone called asking for

you today and that kind of reminded me I should get in touch."

"Who was it?"

"I don't know."

"Don't know?"

"Some woman. Sounded young. Wouldn't give her name. She said she was an old friend of your wife's and she just heard—you know . . . and she wanted to call and say how sorry, and all. Maybe I did the wrong thing, but I told her where you were."

"That's all right. But I can't imagine who . . ."

"I'm not sure, Burt, but I had an idea she was calling long distance. The operator came on first and verified the number. It was a good, clear connection but it—I don't know—had a long distance feel to it. Oh well, what's the difference?"

"A lot of difference. Now I'm interested. What kind of voice?"

"Well, as I said, young. But mature. A nice voice, refined and all that. Very formal, a little cool."

"Uh-huh. I think I get the picture. Thanks, Art."

"Anything I can do for you, Burt?"

"Not a thing. Just keep the mill grinding."

"You're sure, old man? You know how I feel . . . Anything at all."

"Thanks, Art. Just time, that's all. I need lots of time. And listen. I forgot. Thanks for the note and the flowers."

"The very least."

"Right. See you then, Art. The best."

"Soak up the sun. So long."

I hung up, glad that he had signed off. I wanted to get busy acting on that call. Bev had no friends out of town. Only older relatives. And they had all checked in. I had a few old girl friends in New York City, but they were not acquainted with Bev. And anyone we know would have given their name. Besides, I had this hunch. I had mentioned to Alicia where I worked. And she was the kind that somehow would want to know about anyone she associated with.

Down in the office, I looked up her number in the directory. Then, from a phone booth I called long distance and asked for the charge operator. I said I was speaking for Miss Shafton and wanted to know the charges on a call to Buffalo, New York, placed a short time ago. She said she'd call me back but I said I'd hang on. After an age, she located the tab and gave me the charges. Quite satisfied, I went back to my apartment.

In the bathroom I undressed leisurely. There was a small scale next to a clothes hamper. The management had thought of everything. I climbed onto it naked. The dial spun and stopped at 190 pounds. Pleased, I stepped off. A month ago I had weighed two hundred and twelve. Grief beats any diet for losing weight. And, for my age and height, six feet two inches, and my large bone structure, 190 was just about right.

I inspected myself carefully. The pot was gone. My belly was hard and flat. I looked in the mirror. Even the slight puffiness had gone out of my face. I wondered why I cared at all—and at the same moment knew that I was speculating on my attraction for a beauty like Alicia.

A few days before she died, Bev had pleaded with me to go on a diet. "Honestly, Burt," she said one night as I was undressing for bed, "You're the best looking man I think I've ever seen, short of the pretty boy type I can't stand. You're big and tall, you've got a full head of hair with just a nice touch of grey, features all in the right place but sort of rugged too, a six inch smile that won't quit and pretty legs. But, you're fat!"

"Pretty legs!" I said. "Cut it out. Men don't have pretty legs. They just have hairy extensions to walk on."

"Yes they do have pretty legs. No they don't either. But you do. Listen, big pal. Lover. Why don't you take off about twenty pounds? You'd look five or ten years younger, you'd feel better and live longer and I'd have to carry a baseball bat to beat back the fatal females of America."

"Listen! I don't do so bad now. And don't forget it."

"I know. But how about it? Twenty pounds?"

Well, I did start on the diet. And Bev, bless her heart, will never know how she helped me finish it.

Putting on my bathing suit, I decided that she was right. I did look five or ten years younger than my age. And maybe sometime I would know if I felt better. I hurried down to the beach and plunged into the waves. It was while I was floating on my back puzzling Alicia, that I made up my mind not to say anything to her about the call to my office.

She was her best, smiling self when she came to the door. Apparently she was quite satisfied with my credentials as an ordinary guy. And this was the way I wanted it. Only if she was off guard would I have a chance of finding out what she was all about.

She wore some sort of white organdy cocktail dress with a splash here and there of purple flowers. It was without neck or strap and seemed to hold its own without aid from anything but the high, full shelf of her breasts.

"My God," I said. "Maybe I should have worn a dinner jacket instead of a sport coat."

"Come in," she said with a chuckle. "This is a sort of occasion. My first date in this never-never land."

Never-never what? I wanted to say. And wondered if she always wore white as a badge of her purity. "Don't think I'm complaining. I'm crazy about the dress. And this is an occasion for me too."

Dinner was steak and asparagus and a sort of potato and cheese souffle, topped with strawberry shortcake. It was the first meal I managed to finish all the way. We ate it on the patio. One of those huge, orange-neon moons of Florida vintage was abroad over the water. Every star was an etching in silver, and the pale glow of fluorescent lights that shone from the buildings on palms and flowers, gave the whole thing a fairyland atmosphere. It was delightful and for the first time she chatted like an excited little girl. But withal she managed skillfully to circumnavigate every important detail of her life. I decided she was not one you could press. And I waited.

Later we pulled back the rug and danced to the radio. When I suggested there were some full orchestras nearby, she changed the subject so quickly that I didn't bring it up again. At the moment I had forgotten about the phone call she was expecting, and oddly, so had she because she didn't use it as an excuse. I began to think there wasn't going to be any phone call.

She mixed a plentiful round of Manhattans and later highballs. Toward midnight, I was feeling little pain and she was feeling none at all. Apparently she was not an experienced drinker, and this was, as she said, an occasion. It was an occasion for her to anesthetize long stored-up tensions. And these were not ordinary tensions that at times gave her laughter an hysterical sound, like something screaming for relief. These were not only tensions, but welling fears—just this side of terror.

It was while we were dancing in the semi-darkness in that state of alcoholic unreality where music, sound, light and shadow impression, and body sensation fuse into one sensually hynotic mood, that I kissed her. Her body fastened against mine with such desperation that she might have been trying to escape into my being. Her lips pressed so tightly that it was almost pain and I felt the warm shock of her tongue searching my mouth. It was like pushing straight up into a stall and then nosing over into a long dive, spinning out of control.

And when we did come out of it we were on the sofa and I was pushing down on the rim of her dress and she was helping me until with startling clarity, even in the gloom, she was naked to the waist. For a moment I sat in awe, staring at the swollen, white perfection of her breasts, gently sloping and sharply rising, blatantly exposed, aching to be touched as in some tantalizing dream. And then I buried my head in all that warmth and softness, finding more than a physical need. All the pent up wretchedness welled moistly to my eyes.

"Oh, Bev, Bev! Forgive me," I sobbed incoherently. "It's too much to stand."

And all the time Alicia was holding me against her and saying, "I don't care. I don't care what you think of me. I want you. I need you. My God, how I need you!" And in our own way, we were both lost—and found.

I took her to bed then and we said and did things lovers do, not knowing or caring if we loved. And when we were consumed in body we held each other and talked and talked and found another relief. I told for the first time of my agony of loss and she told me she was, "Scared, Burt. Scared, scared. Scared all the time." But never why.

It was after two A.M., and dressed, we were having coffee in the kitchen, stretching and yawning in animal comfort. And then the phone rang, a strident jangle in the tropic whisper of the morning.

I watched her, expecting the reaction of one who is expecting a call. She was lifting the cup to her lips and let it drop with a clatter to the saucer. Her jaw unhinged, her eyes widened toward the sound and the color slowly sneaked out of her face.

"It's only the phone," I said. "Aren't you expecting a call?"

"No," she said. "I . . . No! No!" It was almost a scream.

"Do you want me to get it? Probably a wrong number," I said lamely. I was dumbfounded.

She didn't answer me. In a slow, sleepy motion, she

ran a hand through her hair and walked trance-like into the living room. The ring had sounded perhaps a dozen times and seemed to grow in intensity. She picked up the receiver. "Hel-hel-hello?" Her voice had a timid, uncertain tone, little girl in the dark. "Hel-hello? . . . Hello! Hello!" She listened intently. "For god's sake, who is it! . . . Answer me. An—swer meeee!" This time it *was* a scream.

I thought she was losing her mind. She stayed there listening a full minute. She never moved. Then, slowly she hung up. She came back and slumped into her chair.

"What the hell," I said. "What're you so excited about?"

Her eyes came up to mine slowly. They were glazed —yet she was cold sober. "There was someone . . . There was someone . . . but they wouldn't answer."

"Some character playing a joke," I said.

"No one," she said flatly. "Absolutely no one has this number."

I thought how wrong she was. I had it. "It's in the book," I said.

She seemed now to be under some cold and desperate control. "Yes," she said. "In the book. But not under my real name."

"What *is* your real name?" I said stupidly.

"You don't know what this could mean," she said. "You couldn't possibly know."

"Well, I realize that. But if it's some pest bothering you, maybe I can help."

"Pest!" she said. And the word was full of scorn. "Pest. If only it was a simple thing like that." Then she put out the kitchen light and led me by the hand to the patio. It was washed with moonlight. She stood with me by the rail and looked carefully around the building, then up and down the road. "Listen," she said, "the terrible part is that I can't tell you anything. And yet I've got to have help. Never mind. You go back to your place. This is far, far over your head." I could feel her trembling against me. "You mustn't get involved at any cost. That phone call might be a prank. But I don't think so. Not with what I know. It's more like someone checking to see if I'm here. Go now, before I weaken and change my mind. Oh, God, just get out of here!"

The way she said it made something crawl up my spine and prick my scalp. "Listen, I'm no hero, but there isn't much else that could happen to me. I'm past caring very much. In fact you're the only thing that's happened to me to give me any life at all. I'm going to stick with you awhile anyway."

"I couldn't be that selfish," she moaned. "And I can't tell you anything."

"Never mind. You're in trouble. You're expecting someone to follow up that call. Someone dangerous?"

"Yes."

"I guess I can handle one angry man."

"Maybe not just one."

"My God!"

"You see?"

"No. But I'll take you to my apartment. You can spend the night with me there."

"Oh, would you? Would you!"

"Yes. Of course."

"But I have to know."

"If he comes?"

"Yes. If he—if they come."

"I'll stay here then."

"No. I couldn't let you. But you could watch from somewhere."

"From the beach!"

"Yes. Yes! Oh, God bless you." She tip-toed away and in a moment reappeared like a shadow beside me. She pressed something big and steel hard into my hand.

I looked at it in the moonlight, knowing what it was—a .45 caliber automatic.

"Jesus!" I said. "What a cannon for a little girl. This must be *real* trouble."

"I'll tell you this much and no more," she said.

I waited. She was silent a long moment before she said, "I . . . I . . . how shall I put it? Well, this way. I am the key to something so valuable that all the dishonest and maybe a few of the honest people in the country would be looking for me if they knew. And the ones who do know would torture or murder me for it. Now take me to your place. Quick! Hurry!"

She darted into the bedroom and came out in a moment with a big suitcase. "Take this. I have some things packed. I may need them. Now look outside."

I crept around the breezway and looked below. It was well enough lighted to see. There was no one. I came back. I hurried her with the suitcase to my apartment. I kissed her quickly. "Lock the door. I can watch both places from the beach. I'm the craziest damn fool in the world. But what have I got to lose? Hang on." I left.

I went down the back stairs and crept along for a ways behind buildings. Then I headed for the beach and circled back along the water's edge and inland on my belly to where I could see.

I took the forty-five out of my pocket. I checked. There was a full clip. I slid a round into the chamber and pulled the hammer back to half cock. In the dim overhead lights of the breezeway above, I could see both doors. I waited, listening to the lonely sound of the surf.

CHAPTER THREE

DURING THE MORNING HOURS, I had a couple of bad scares
when, at intervals, two cars pulled quietly up to the
building. But they were only couples returning from
parties or late drinking bouts at bars or nightclubs. They
disappeared in their apartments and all was quiet again.
After that it was a downhill struggle against sleep.

When dawn came and there had been not a sign of
trouble, not a movement around either door, I closed
my eyes a moment to relieve the ache of watching. The
moment became two hours and when I awoke the sun
was already bright in the sky and it was after eight
o'clock. I had been lying on my belly with my head
cradled on one arm, the gun, still at half cock, clutched
tightly in one extended fist. I pulled my head up sharply,
spitting sand. I had that awful feeling of being too late,
like the night they took me to Bev and there was nothing left for me but the sad identification.

I sneaked the .45 into my pocket, feeling foolish and
wondering at what a strange sight I would be had anyone taking an early dip come upon me. But, though an
occasional car passed along the ocean road, the beach
was deserted. I brushed away sand and smoothed some
of the wrinkles from my clothes. I walked slowly toward
the Tropic Moon.

It was a time of morning when the sun was all light
and not much heat, the air not yet humid, but crisp and
salty. It was a time of stillness, the virgin beginning of

the day, unspoiled by human sound or movement. It was far too peaceful to make a reality of the crazy dread of the night before. I felt like someone had played a very bad and very impractical joke on me. In the quiet sanity of the morning, Alicia's fears seemed like the posturing of a child over shadows. I wasn't at all sure I had taken her to my apartment and would find her in my bed. And yet I couldn't shake a certain feeling that I had to hurry —that it was *too* quiet.

I was standing at my door, getting out my key, when this big grey Lincoln pulled to the curb. The man who climbed out of it was big, too. And alone. I guess it was the uncertain way he squinted up at the building that kept me waiting there with the key already in the lock. I knew he didn't belong. He saw me too and must have been aware that I was watching him. But after a quick glance in my direction, he turned away with something like disdain, the way you look at a mere bird in the sky. After all, it's only a bird.

He began to peer at doors below, looking for name cards. His movements were easy and almost casual and yet there was this attitude of superb confidence and knowing about him that gave him, well . . . power. That's the only word I can think of that explains him. Powerful. It was like some slow, patient force had been set loose in him and nothing would turn it back. Funny how you feel things like that. Even at a distance. It backs up what I said awhile ago. People have an aura about them.

Well, I wasn't at all surprised when he came up the stairs in that loose-moving way, like a big, amiable bloodhound wagging his tail but never losing the scent. And I wasn't surprised when he found Alicia's door and began ringing the bell. I let him ring awhile, thinking he would go away. But he didn't. He leaned against the railing and calmly waited.

I stuck my hand in my pocket and let it tighten around

the pistol grip and walked over. He was about six-four, lean, wide-shouldered and raw-boned as some Texans, though he wasn't the type for a ten-gallon hat. He had a rather long, craggy face that ended in a mountain of jaw. He looked in his middle forties. His hair was grey-brown, combed straight back from a high, rugged forehead, and he was deeply tanned, as though he was born under the sun. He was impeccably dressed in an expensively cut, blue gabardine, hand-painted tie and silk shirt as white as a fresh tablecloth at the Ritz. One great hand came up to his face, and, with a bored deliberateness, rubbed his cheek, setting off a shower of sun sparks from what looked like ten thousand dollar's worth of diamond on his finger.

"Looking for Miss Shafton?" I asked casually, feeling neither tough nor capable, in spite of the .45 in my pocket.

He turned slowly and studied me with eyes that were as cool and grey as a San Francisco fog, yet impersonal and without malice.

"That's right," he said. His wide, thin mouth had a look of faint amusement.

"She's gone."

"I'll wait."

"No use. She won't be back."

The amusement lingered on his face like the cool fog in his eyes. "How would you know? You her father?"

There was no use getting mad at him. I sensed that right away. It would be like getting mad at a rock because it hit you. He was that impersonal—and placid. "All right. So she's around. But she's not seeing anyone. Give me your name. I'll tell her you were here."

He reached inside his coat and I tensed. But he only brought out a long, white envelope. "When you go back to your apartment," he said evenly, "give her this." He handed me the envelope. He jerked a thumb toward the street. "I'll be waiting in my car. In case she might want to see me." He walked away, down the steps with the same mixture of good-humored disdain and confidence.

I watched him for a moment before it came to me to wonder how he knew she was in my apartment. Alicia was right when she said I was in over my head. I felt like an ass because I had sweated there all night on the beach. He must have watched her go to my apartment. But then why hadn't he gone there in the first place?

Alicia awoke slowly, then quickly with startled eyes. She looked at her watch and pulled the sheet around her—as though there were still something to conceal. I gave her the envelope without a word.

"What's this?" And when I didn't say anything, she opened it. There was nothing inside but the jagged half of a bill and a small key. It meant nothing to me. But it was the lighted fuse to some time bomb inside her. "Where did you get this!" She said it with the utmost excitement but apparently without fear.

"He's outside in his car," I said. "Waiting."

She examined the key carefully. It was small but extremely heavy for its size, as though made for a strong and important lock. She fumbled in her purse and brought out a similar key. She put them together. They matched. At least they were of the same stock—but the webs were different. She smiled and looked up at me like it was the key to Fort Knox. Next, she took the bill and examined it as carefully. It was half of a hundred-dollar bill. The edges were jagged where it was severed. The bill had not been torn, but cut apart, as if with some clever tool that made an intricate design. Again she reached in her purse, this time bringing out the other half of the bill. She placed them together and they matched perfectly.

"What is he like?" she said with mounting urgency.

I described him. She simply nodded her head as though his description fitted with one she had heard but not from any former meeting. It was the damnedest thing I ever saw. Then she hopped out of bed and seemed not to notice that she was naked except for her panties. She dressed quickly. She put the envelope with the bill in her purse.

"I'll be back in a little while," she said. "I've been waiting for this but I never thought . . . Anyway, I won't be very long."

"Are you sure it's all right?"

"All right!" she almost shouted. "It's the end of this whole thing." She smiled. "And the beginning, too. Of something else."

"Don't you want me to stick close?"

"No. I'll be perfectly safe. Wait for me, and maybe I'll explain." And then she was gone——out the door, down the steps. I saw her climb into the Lincoln and drive away.

I hesitated. And then on impulse, I ran down to my own car and shoved off after them.

CHAPTER FOUR

IT WAS NO problem getting them in range and then keeping well back. They weren't moving fast. Somehow I had expected them to be tearing away at high speed, Alicia kidnapped or both of them hastening to hatch some plot, some super con game. But they drove as though to a picnic and the bright, sleepy day denied everything but lazy pleasure and tropic joy while most of the nation froze under dreary skies.

I had plenty of time to wonder why I was following

them at all. It was really none of my business, though Alicia had involved me to a certain extent and I had invested a night's sleep and not a little worry.

The real reason, however, had nothing to do with these things. I had been more lonely than I dared admit before Alicia and this new turn of events was a threat to my small reprieve. If Alicia should suddenly disappear, I would return to what? Nothing. A void. I had to keep moving. I had to fill my life with action. Any kind of action so long as it kept me from morbid thinking and self-pity.

I followed them down to the little town of Ft. Lauderdale, where they stopped at a bank. I parked and watched from a careful distance. They were on the street again in about fifteen minutes. Alicia was smiling. The man looked purposeful and, for the first time, in a hurry. Alicia showed him a small square of paper which he looked at briefly before she dropped it in her purse. The whole thing had the nature of an exchange. At least of information.

At first, when they went into the bank, I got to thinking about those keys and the possibility of a safety deposit box. But the keys had a homemade look and resembled no deposit box keys I had ever seen. Also I had noticed that when she put them together, they matched only in size and stock, the groovings, called the bit or web, were different, indicating there were two locks. The bank holds the key to the second lock on a deposit box, the depositor keys for only one lock. Of course, there could have been two deposit boxes, but I didn't think so.

The big man opened the door for Alicia, slid quickly behind the wheel and gunned away. I managed to keep them in sight, weaving around traffic, turning corners tightly for several blocks. But the big boy with the cool eyes and the casual manner drove with all the casualness of a man late for the last train home. And then I caught a red light with traffic already in the intersection. I lost them.

I stayed in my apartment all day and hated myself for worrying. And as much for waiting. Yet there was this fragile link between us, this sharing of a bed and a small understanding. There was this mixture in her of willful independence and little girl lost. I flattered myself that she needed me for all her front. And I needed her. I needed somone. God! How I needed someone. And beyond the independence and the girl-lostness, there was the excitement of her. She was excitement and excitement followed her. She attracted it. She was terrified and a little in love with her terror, like someone who races fearfully into a whirlpool when all around it the waters are calm.

Dusk crept across a pale sky like a stealthy shadow of the night that followed close behind. Flood lights sprang up at the base of buildings like amber flowers night-blooming on cue. Soon after, headlights burst around a corner and sprayed the terrace below. A car door slammed, the lights flew backward and she came up the steps, pausing to watch the car out of sight. I waited in the darkness, watching from my window. She looked hesitantly in my direction, so I flipped the light switch and she came to my door and knocked.

There was a terribly subdued look about her when she came in. She crumpled in, if you could call it that.

"Well?" I said.

"Get me a drink," she said. "Please!"

She wouldn't say a word until she had swallowed two jiggers of bourbon on the rocks. She sat slumped in a chair, her head bent down. When she looked up there was the same glaze of terror in her eyes I had seen once before. When that phone rang in the middle of the night. There was more than terror. She looked in a panic.

"What now?" I asked.

She gulped smoke down her lungs and exhaled. "He's dead."

"Who's dead?"

"Emory. Ralph—Ralph Emory. The man who was here today."

"How could he be dead?"

"I can't . . . I can't even tell it."

"From the beginning. Before I'll believe it. I thought that was he who drove up with you just now."

"No. Oh, my God, Burt. Help me. Help me!"

"Get under control and tell it. Then we'll see." She must be telling the truth or she was the best damned actress I ever saw. And if she was, it would be murder. I was certain. Excitement is one thing, murder another. Mentally I had already packed my bags and was long gone. But I had to hear.

"He was shot right before my eyes. It was so . . . I can't even . . ."

"Start from when you left here."

"We . . . we drove to . . . I mean toward Miami. Over a back road. A truck route, I think."

"You went directly from here?" If she lied about that, well . . .

"Yes. No, not directly. We stopped for a few minutes at a bank in Ft. Lauderdale."

Well, she wasn't lying about that! "Go on," I said.

"We were speeding down this deserted back road. And . . . and then a big sedan pulled across the road up ahead and stopped. We thought it had stalled. We slowed just in time. There were three men in the car. They were dressed like . . . well, like they were going fishing. I don't know where I got that idea, except that they wore rough clothes and one of them had on a yachting cap. He was sort of barrel-chested and chunky looking. He had a big smile on his face. 'Motor conked out just as we were makin' a turn,' he said. 'Isn't that silly?

Give us a hand, will you?' There was, you know, nothing sinister about him. He spoke very well. Very friendly.

"Emory got out and walked over. The other two men began to push. Then the man with the yachting cap reached in the front seat and brought out a gun. He motioned Emory in the car. Emory started to obey and then suddenly he kicked this man in the . . . in the . . ."

"Groin?"

"Yes. And when the man doubled over, Emory grabbed the gun and turned it on the other two. But they had the trunk open in that split second and they both came up with rifles. Emory fired, and at almost the same time one of the rifles went off. He . . . he . . . Emory, that is, stood there for the longest time and then he . . . he fell in a heap and rolled over."

"Where was he hit?"

"In . . . he . . . there was blood all over his face. The temple, I think. It was horrible beyond any description. Like watching an execution. Two of them began loading him in the car and the one who had been kicked came to get me. That's when I finally woke up. The motor was running so I slid over and headed right for him. I turned sharply, but caught him lightly with the mud guard. I went into a ditch and came out again onto the road. I almost turned over. I was doing a hundred inside a minute. I heard what sounded like shots. I can't be sure.

"I went around a bend and took a side road back to the main highway. I watched in the mirror but they . . . I never saw them again. I took the car to Mr. Emory's house—I knew where he lived. His man, butler or whatever, brought me home. I didn't tell him anything—just that Mr. Emory met some friends and asked me to bring the car back. Friends!" she said bitterly. "I . . . I don't think they intended to kill him. But they . . . they did.

Right . . . right before . . ." She broke off with a sob and began to cry.

I let her cry it out and then I said, "Now, where were you going at the time?"

"To pick up something at the airport in Miami."

"What?" I asked sharply.

"A suitcase."

"And what's in the suitcase?"

"A box. A heavy metal box."

"Sure. And what's in the box?"

"It's locked. It has two outside locks. You open them and then there's another lid and it has two combination dials you have to work before you open it. I was about to sell the box to Emory for . . . for two hundred thousand dollars."

"My God! And what in the name of hell is in it?"

"That's it," she said. "That's the awful thing about it. I don't know."

"You don't *know?*"

"No. I never have known."

I was dumb with unbelief. We just sat there looking at each other.

CHAPTER FIVE

"ALL RIGHT," I said. "If I'm going to believe the rest of it, I'll have to believe this, too."

"It doesn't matter if you believe me or not," she said sadly. "It won't change anything—now. If it weren't for Emory, I . . . I mean, what happened, I wouldn't have mentioned the box at all. But I had to talk to someone."

"Let's start over again. You don't know what's in the box; you never have."

"No."

"And yet it's so valuable, someone was willing to pay almost a quarter of a million for it."

"Yes. Actually its worth far more than that to the right person. Its worth is incalculable."

"How can you possibly say that if you don't know what's in it?"

"I was told."

"What's in it?"

"No. About its worth."

"God! I'm getting more and more confused. Tell me where you got it and from whom. The whole story."

"The more I tell you, the more involved you become. Why do you want to get mixed up in something that's already killed one man? And with me almost a total stranger to you?"

"I don't know," I said. "Maybe I have a subconscious desire to commit suicide." I said it with a chuckle but in a way I knew it was true.

"Look, Burt," she said earnestly. "I'm . . . I'm wrung dry, nervous and confused myself. Nothing makes much sense to me but . . ."

"Nothing makes sense to *you*. Huh. That's a laugh."

"But it does seem to me," she hurried on, "that you ought to consider not so much how you feel now, but how you'll feel in the future—in a month, a year. Right now you think your whole world is shot and the hell with tomorrow. You're lonely and your life is empty and the first girl who comes along—me—who gives you a little sympathy and understanding—well, you want to fall off a cliff with me. But a year, even a month, can patch up a lot of bruises. You'll look back and be glad you didn't get into this nightmare."

I looked at her sitting there slumped in her chair,

seeming suddenly frail and helpless, her tear-streaked face, red and blotchy, the coolness gone from her eyes. And she was far more beautiful and desirable than on the first day I saw her. And I thought, that was a pretty little speech but you said the wrong thing if you want to get rid of me. Because now, I'm also beginning to *like* you. Still . . . all the good actresses aren't on the stage. And all the good psychologists don't have offices with diplomas on the wall.

"Thanks," I said. "But don't give me that platitude about time heals all wounds. When something goes dead inside you, it's dead. Period. Time just makes it easier to walk around practising *looking* alive." I really felt that way about it.

She shrugged. "Well," she said. "I tried. I put a little salve on my conscience. But I'm not so brave and strong that I want to suffer alone if someone's fool enough to bathe in my hot water. I'll let you think awhile. I'm exhausted. I'm dead."

"To look at you, I would guess you would have all the help you wanted. Isn't there anyone?"

"No. Not now. Not for a long time. And certainly not here."

"Well, with two hundred thousand you can run a long way."

"To Mars if I had transportation. But I wonder if even that would be far enough—now. I don't have the money yet. And I may never get it."

"Why?"

"Because we didn't complete the deal before Emory was killed."

"And if you had?"

"I'd give the money to his wife."

"She's honest, too."

"Don't be so sure about that. There are a lot of loose ends that might lead to some very dirty garbage. And

I've been willing to close my mind—for two hundred thousand."

"And now?"

"I can't say I don't still want the money. But Emory's dead. And what I tried to sell him, killed him. I can't hide from that one. Burt. Oh, Burt. What shall I do?"

"I'll tell you what I'd do. I'd find out what's in that box. And after I had a good, careful look, I might want to have a little talk with the police. Does anyone know where you are now?"

"No. That was Emory who phoned. He wanted to make sure I was here, but he didn't want to talk to me except in person. You can see that he had reason to be careful."

"And what about the box? Is there a possibility that anyone knows where it is?"

"Anything is possible. But it's not probable. I think those men were going to try to force Emory to tell."

"He didn't have any clue in his pockets."

"No. I had it."

"The dirty bastards. He didn't seem like such a bad guy. And he was a man!"

"I didn't really know him. Even so . . . it's awful."

"Do you think you could get the box without much danger?"

"I don't know. Sometimes I wonder if it isn't dangerous just thinking about it. It makes me shudder."

"You *have* seen it."

"Yes. I've seen it. That's all."

"So you don't know what's in the box. And you want to sell it. But now you don't have anyone to sell it to."

"Well, that's not necessarily true. Emory has some kind of partner or associate who would be willing to buy it. But I'm afraid to pick it up. If those men were cruising around, they might recognize me."

"Do you know the name of the other man you could sell it to? Where he could be reached?"

"No. But Mrs. Emory would be able to tell me."

"Why didn't you talk to her when you went back to Emory's house?"

"I tried. But she wasn't in. Now I'm afraid to go any-where."

I knew she was hinting at something and I was pretty sure what it was. So I said, "I suppose you want me to get the box for you."

"That would be asking a lot."

"You're telling me." I liked her. But not that much.

"I wouldn't want you to do it for nothing," she said.

Now I was curious. "What would you want me to do it for?"

She considered. "I'll give you a thousand dollars cash to pick it up. It won't be dangerous for you because no one is looking for you and no one would connect you with the box."

"If it isn't dangerous, why is it worth a thousand?"

"Well, of course there is always a remote possibility you could run into some kind of trouble. It isn't exactly a simple little errand."

"And what happens after I get it?"

Again she was thoughtful. "If you can arrange the sale of it for me, I'll give you ten percent."

"Ten percent? Of two hundred thousand?"

She nodded.

"Wow! That's twenty thousand dollars."

"Yes," she said. "It would be worth that to me. I can't handle it alone. Not anymore."

Well, I wasn't broke by any means. But twenty-one thousand dollars is a lot of loot. It would probably take me ten years to save that kind of money out of my salary. Besides, I was in a frame of mind where I didn't give a particular damn what happened to me. I wanted to fill my life with distractions and this seemed, at the time, like an exciting game with big stakes. "All right," I said, "I'll pick up the box. But if I don't like the smell of what's inside, the rest of the deal is off."

She went in the bedroom and came back counting bills. She handed me a wad. "Here's five hundred," she said. "As long as this is a business proposition, I'll give you the rest when you bring me the box."

I counted the money and put it in my pocket.

"About the rest of the deal," she said, "I'm not sure."

"Why?"

"Because we'll never know what's in the box. Never."

"Why? If we have it here, we . . ."

"It can't be opened."

"You don't have the keys or the combination?"

"I have the keys but not the combinations. There are two. Only Emory could figure them. They were in a code. I have part of it and he had the other part."

"So what? We'll force it open."

She shook her head. "Unh-uh. You'll never know how cleverly this was worked out. It just can't be forced. I would have tried."

"How come?"

"You've heard of booby traps that go off when you tamper with them—explode?"

"Of course. I was in the war. You don't mean to tell me . . ."

"Yes. Exactly that. A kind of super booby trap."

"Oh, now wait a minute. You believe that fairy tale?"

"Yes. Positively. Because I know the man who built it. He's probably lied to a lot of people. But not to me. There's only one way into that box and that's with the combinations."

"It could be soaked in water."

"Waterproof."

"How about a man who's good with locks, say a top-notch safe cracker?"

"He thought of that, too. And don't ask me how he got around it. I don't know."

"All right. Who's the man?"

"He was my husband."

That rocked me for a moment. "You should know him then. We're talking all around this thing. If you want company in this mess, you'd better tell me about him and the box."

"After you get it."

"In Miami at the airport?"

"Yes."

"It's checked?"

"Yes. Eastern Airlines." She brought a ticket from her purse. She handed it to me. "Here. This is the claim check. It's in a small black suitcase."

At the door she kissed me. She was very tender. "Hurry, Burt. And whatever you do, if . . . if you don't plan to come back, for the love of God, don't tamper with that box."

CHAPTER SIX

I TOOK THE MAIN HIGHWAY to Miami, Route 1. There was quite a lot of traffic and I had to pass through two or three small towns, which made the going slow. But, remembering Emory, the last thing I wanted was anything resembling a back road. And the busy swirl of traffic with its multi-colored license plates from a dozen or more states, the lights of store windows and gas stations, gave me a feeling of security.

I had no particular dread, on the other hand. I was driving an unknown car, I was not connected with Alicia or the box so far as anyone but Emory and Alicia were concerned. Emory couldn't talk and Alicia wouldn't. At least, it was fantastic to suppose she would have any reason to. No, I was not very alarmed, although I realized the possibilities for trouble were infinite. I figured that if there were trouble, it would come after we had the box, if at all, and I could worry about that later. As long as Emory didn't drift into my mind, I was immensely excited and about as curious as you can get. No matter what Alicia said so dogmatically about the box, I had a smug conviction that it could be opened and that, by God, I *would* open it and see what was worth all that money and a man's life. I was wondering why Emory wouldn't tell Alicia what was in the box, because certainly he knew, and a half dozen unanswerables, when I reached the airport.

It was then that I had my first uncomfortable feeling of doubt and fear, and I parked the car near an easy exit and in such a way that it couldn't be blocked. As a last gesture to caution, I backed it into the diagonal space so that I would have to delay maneuvering around. I cut the lights and turned the key in the ignition. Then, as an afterthought, I started the motor again and left it running. Next I rolled up the windows, got out and observed the car from a few feet away. I couldn't see any exhaust smoke and I couldn't hear the motor. The car looked as locked and silent as the one next to it. Right then I thanked God for that new, sweet-running engine and for the guys who invented silent valves.

Walking into the airport I felt better. It was a little thing and perhaps a foolish risk, but seconds can save you in a jam. Besides, how long would it take to claim a piece of baggage? But what a piece of baggage it was!

The waiting room was the usual scene of activity mixed with boredom. The activity came from blaring speakers announcing arrivals and departures, porters lugging suitcases, taxi drivers looking for fares, passengers trickling to and from plane gates and counter clerks doing the things they do with tickets and reservation lists. The boredom came from waiting, as it always does, the dull-eyed customers squatting in their seats, restless behind newspapers and magazines.

I found Eastern Airlines and in a moment I had spotted the checkroom. There were two or three people waiting their turn. It was the most ordinary scene. Inside a minute or two, I would have the case with its astonishing box and be gone. But as a precaution, I bought a newspaper and took a seat where I could casually place everyone in the room in a safe category.

I spent a few seconds on the headlines and sub-captions, looking for a splash about Emory. At a quick glance there was nothing on the first, second and third pages, so I found a crossword puzzle, made fake stabs at working it, now and then looking up with a thoughtful expression that covered the room section by section. I couldn't find anyone who looked in the least sinister or out of place, except for one rather rugged looking guy in a tan sport jacket. I spent too much time on him because he kept watching the door. And then a thin, ash blonde with a blotchy, over-painted face joined him and they hurried off, probably to some waiting plane.

That was when I got up and walked over to the check stand. There was a bald-headed little man with a string bean ten-year-old girl on his arm, and a Cuban couple making Cuban sounds at each other, flashing white teeth in dark faces. They were all gone with their stuff in less than ninety seconds that seemed more than ninety minutes. The place was air-conditioned, but I could feel the sweat beading under my shirt while I stood there attempting to personify bored unconcern, wanting to swing around suddenly to catch some watcher off guard —a sure giveaway.

Calmly I took the check out of my pocket and gave

it to the attendant. I don't know why I expected this would be a major event for him, too, that he would look startled or wary, sound an alarm, the color drain from his face, something like that. But the check failed to excite him in any way. He gave it a quick, deadpan look and disappeared in an ocean of leather. He came back in a moment with a square, black bag, a little larger than a hat box. I gave him a dollar and when I didn't bother with change, that *did* excite him. I saw his eyes widen, and turned away before it came to me that that was my first mistake. Generosity at a check stand is rare—and also remembered.

The bag was unduly heavy for its size. But I had expected that. I didn't exactly swing it around. I clutched the handle until my nails dug my palms and held it rigid against my thigh. I kept remembering what she said about the box being wired. It was one thing to talk about it and another to be carrying it around.

I moved slowly, sauntered to the exit. At the door I had a vast sense of relief. There was a stocky looking guy leaning against the wall. He was giving me a speculative look. That bothered me plenty for a moment—until I saw that he wore one of those visored caps, and said, "Taxi, mister? Anywhere in Miami for a buck."

I shook my head. "No thanks," I muttered. I had my hand on the door when I suddenly froze. He was speaking again, and at the same time I was seeing the image of that cap he wore, and matching it with Alicia's words. "One of them had on a yachting cap. He was barrel-chested and chunky looking. They wore rough clothes, like they were going fishing."

And the cap *this* one wore had a gold crest—a coil of rope and an anchor. He was also chunky, barrel-chested and wore faded blue jeans. "Say, friend," he was calling. "Got a light? I'm fresh out."

I was about to push on as though I didn't hear him, but he spoke with a booming, false heartiness you couldn't miss unless you were deaf. Also, it came to me then that he probably didn't know me. He was checking everyone as they went by. If I ignored him I would be mighty suspicious.

I turned around and ordered my face to look friendly. "Sure, buddy," I said. I set the bag down casually between my legs, gripping it tightly with my heels. He had a cigarette in his hand, bringing it up to his beefy face. He was smiling. That is, the lower half of his face was smiling. The upper half was as still and cold as rigor mortis.

I took out my lighter and flicked it. My thumb was sweating on the striker arm and slipped. It gave a feeble spark and wouldn't light. An agony of time went by while I tried again. I could feel my legs shaking against the case. But next flip it worked. He bent his head into the flame. He stayed there too long after the cigarette was lighted. I saw that he was using the time to study the case. I looked down. I had not taken time to inspect the case closely. Now I saw that it clearly bore the gold, engraved initials, *G. M.*, the same ones that were on Alicia's brief case. I was instantly as aware as if I had read his mind, that this had meaning for him.

He lifted his head slowly and I was looking into his eyes. They were as dead as before. Only his smile had changed. It hovered on his face, flickering like a candle in the wind. And then went out. His hand crept into one roomy pocket of his faded trousers. And Alicia had the .45!

"I'll take that bag to your car, mister," he said softly. "It looks heavy."

I wasn't sure I heard him right. Maybe I didn't want to believe that's what he said. "What was that?" I croaked. "I don't get you, buddy?"

"Sonofabitch." It was almost a whisper. "You heard me. Gimme that bag!"

"Oh," I said. "You wanna carry it for me. Sure." I

picked it up, began to hand it to him, raised it quickly and jammed it in his face. It was much later that I thought how it might have exploded in my hands.

He fell backwards. Blood was beginning to spurt out of his nose. I didn't wait to ask him if he wanted a band-aid. I shot out the door. It wasn't far and I was under the gun of fear like nothing I had experienced, except when we swarmed the beaches at Saipan.

I yanked the door open and flung the bag in back. It clanked dangerously against the seat. In two swift motions I pushed down on both buttons that lock the doors. I had seen them running, the big guy in front, two close behind. They swarmed the car, yanking at the doors. The motor was still running. I had only to flip in drive. I burned rubber and swung in a wide arc out the near exit. I careened left instead of right, the way I had come. Some instinct told me not even to give away the right direction.

There are few cars with as much acceleration as an Olds. And I was jamming it to the floor boards. It was the closest thing to flying without being airborne. Yet, when I checked the mirror, the hard glare of lights were already coming after me. I shot around a bend and took the first side road right. I was in some sort of housing development. They didn't miss. They made the turn about a quarter mile behind.

Houses fled past like lighted telephone poles and still managed to look snug and safe. It was a narrow road. The car rocked dangerously. There were taillights ahead. I had to slow because when I pulled out to pass there were on-coming headlights. The mirror warned that now they were gaining fast. I took a chance. I slammed into passing gear and shot around the car ahead. The horn of the on-coming car blared its anger and then bleated fear. Headlights exploded at me through the windshield. I yanked the wheel right. Brakes squealed from the car abreast and falling back. I was too short and knew it. There was a sickening thud as my bumper caught his fender, then ripped on through. And I was free. And safe. But only from collision. I'd worry about the guy's fender later.

The maneuver gave me a little time. I rocketed ahead again. I made another right. Their lights disappeared. I made another right, canting, almost rolling, then falling back. I flung madly up the street. There were cross streets but I had an idea. I watched the houses out of the corner of my eye. Another half block and I found it. A dark one. I looked. Nothing behind. I braked hard. The wheels locked. I skidded. Then I turned—into the dark driveway.

There was an open garage. I cut the lights and pulled into it in the dark. I struck the back wall, but not hard. I sat waiting, bursting for air, like before you come to the surface after a deep dive. I turned around and watched through the rear window. Lights approached. They bobbed and weaved crazily. That was good. They were under full throttle. They droned past, a dark shadow behind a shower of light. Then I exhaled.

In ten minutes they were back. The lights came steadily this time. They were cruising. I was in the garage looking out a side window. I had closed the garage door the minute they were gone. The lights had an odd look, as though one headlight was twisted sideways. Then I got it. They had a searchlight and were playing it on the driveways. I ducked down.

A cone of light fingered the window above my head and splashed against the ceiling. It lingered forever, then walked on. I was in no hurry to leave. This was a kind of determination I had never crossed. It was frightening, relentless. It wasn't going to give up. And it didn't. In the next hour that searchlight looked in my window about every fifteen minutes. It was going on ten o'clock. And all the time I prayed the people in that house were out on the wildest, longest toot of their lives.

And then after awhile they didn't come back. I waited another hour and began to think about getting out of there. And then I waited another hour. Sometime after midnight I crept out of the garage and sneaked to the street. Most of the lights along the block were out. The street was deserted and silent. An offshore wind teased palms that seemed to wear stars in their fronds. It was tropic warm and whispering quiet. It didn't seem like a place of trouble. And I was deceived. I decided to sprint for home.

It was when I turned back to the garage that I heard the voices. They were at the house next door. They were making a block by block, house by house search, approaching from the rear. Once I saw the wink of a flashlight.

I raced to the backyard and lay prone behind some tall vegetation. I watched.

They approached the garage door and I heard one mumble, "Couldn't be here. Skip it." I saw him give the door an upward heave, then quit. I had turned the handle that bolts the door in place and climbed back through the side window. He didn't realize the door wasn't locked. Thank God!

They passed within three feet of me across the lawn, their voices subdued, but audible. "Maybe the girl lives around here," one said. "She could be hiding him. Let's have a look in the garage window." They pulled up a moment and hesitated. "Hell with it," another said. "Come on. Keep moving." He must have been the leader. They obeyed. He was the chunky one, the black visor of his cap visible in the moonlight as they moved on.

I waited another hour. Then I checked the street. It looked and sounded clear. I backed the car out without lights. I turned in the opposite direction from which they had gone. I drove nearly a mile blacked out. I came to the main highway and didn't sight them. I flicked on the lights and sped home.

I pulled up in front of the Tropic Moon. I took the black case under a street light and looked at it. It felt heavy. It looked innocent. It wasn't. Even if there was nothing in it at all, it was far from innocent. It had killed a man.

There was still a light in my apartment. I carried the case up the stairs to Alicia.

CHAPTER SEVEN

ALICIA SAW ME from the window. She opened the door. I placed the black case on the floor. She didn't even look at it. She put her arms around me and held me in silence. Then she said, "I didn't think you'd ever be back. And I was scared. And utterly lonely. When you didn't come and it was past midnight, I . . ."

"It got complicated," I said. Her face looked drawn and tired. I kissed her. "I wonder how we'd react to each other in different circumstances, Alicia."

"Do you think we'll ever get a chance to find out?"

"Not the way it's going. Well, there's your box."

She looked at it for one fascinated moment and shuddered. "It's not mine and never was." She turned away from it and I think she actually was repulsed.

I went to the kitchen alcove and made a couple of stiff ones. She took a long gulp, fell into a chair and said, "Now tell me about it." I did.

"What an ordeal!" she said. "I'm terribly sorry. And now they'll remember you."

"Let's take a look at the box," I said. She just stared at me solemnly, so I got the case and set it down at my feet. "What does G. M. stand for?"

"George McCabe. My husband. He's dead now. I can't prove it, but I know the box killed him. Not literally, of course. Not in the same way it did Emory."

"Then it's high time someone got into it." I unlatched the case and opened it. There was nothing inside but the box. It was gunmetal grey, about a foot and a half square and a foot deep. It looked formidable. I lifted it carefully and held it on my lap. It was heavy.

The box was perfectly plain, except for a carrying handle set in the top of the lid like a tool case. Two locks secured either end of the lid at the front. They were not padlocks. The locks were inset.

Except for its ruggedness, there was nothing very impressive about the thing. But as I sat staring at it, I had the oddest feeling of unease. The more I looked at it, the more uncomfortable I became. Of course it was my imagination working on all that I had heard, but it seemed to breathe and swell in my hands. "Let me have your keys a minute, Alicia."

She gave them to me from her purse. "How come you had these and not Emory?"

"He hadn't yet given me the money—so I held the keys."

"Well, that was a small help anyway." I tried the right lock and found I had the wrong key. I switched to the left lock. It opened easily. I opened the other lock and looked at Alicia.

"Go ahead," she said. "For all the good it will do."

I lifted the lid gingerly. It was like a box within a box, one welded to the other, the inner box slightly smaller. I was looking down at two numbered dials set in the top of the second box. "Two dials, huh?"

She nodded. "There are two combinations. I have one

part of the code, Emory had the other. My part makes no sense at all."

"What kind of code is it?"

"There is just one column of three digit figures. Numbers like 328, 564, 786. I don't get it. Here—I'll show you." She handed me a white square of cardboard with a typewritten column of numbers.

I studied it. "It's too much for me," I said. "But probably quite simple if you have the rest of it. Your husband had a tricky mind."

"His mind was more than tricky," she said. "It was downright clever."

I twirled the dials idly. Feeling foolish, I put my ear to the box and was rewarded with silence.

"Did you think it was a time bomb?" Alicia asked, smiling.

"Hardly. I suppose I was listening for some kind of mechanism though. Just looking at it is disappointing. It doesn't tell me a thing except that it's not going to open with my understanding of these things. And if you could find someone to open it without exploding it, of course he'd get to know what was in it. And who could you trust? I'll have to give this a lot of thought. Because, even if you didn't quite believe it couldn't be opened without blowing up in your face, how could you be sure? It's a chance you just couldn't take. Very ingenious." I closed the box and relocked it. Then I put it back in the case. "What do you want me to do with this for the time being?"

"That's a problem. Why don't you keep it here until we decide."

I put the case in the back of a closet and piled my own luggage on top of it. I came back again and sat down. "Let's see if we can find a clue by discussing your husband. What did he do for a living?"

"Well, there are a lot of things I don't know about him. About his past. He was vague when he spoke of it. But when I married him, he worked for a brokerage firm in Washington, D. C. That's where we lived during the three years we were together. But mostly, I found this out later, George was a gambler. He gambled on the stock market, on horses, cards, dice—anything at all. He was a regular walking Lloyds of London. It was a disease with him. I found it out too late. There was never any happy medium. We were either broke or loaded, depending on his luck. Sometimes it was so bad I had to go to work. Sometimes he disappeared for days. He never told me where he had been. I imagined at some marathon poker game. I knew it wasn't another woman. In spite of himself, he was as in love with me as a sixteen year old in a pink cloud. I suppose that was why I forgave him many times when I was on the brink of leaving him."

"Well," I said. "That doesn't tell us much, except that he might have been cooking this thing up while he was away. You don't suppose he discovered some pocket radar device to control roulette wheels?"

She smiled. "Anything is possible. But the key must be in his past."

"He must have said something about it, even if he lied."

"Oh, yes. But he spoke in generalities and I never pressed him. He was a guard in a bank and . . ."

"Mmmmm, that could lead most anywhere."

"And a guard in one of the government buildings where his father worked. I think it had something to do with the Treasury Department, and what his father did was some kind of secret, though his father died about two and a half years after we were married and George still never mentioned it. He was not the kind you could get information out of until he was good and ready."

"Well, didn't you meet his father?"

"Yes. When we were married, and once after that."

"Only once?"

"Yes. I gathered he wasn't on very good terms with his father in later years. Probably because of his gambling. So we didn't visit him. His mother was dead."

"And his father never mentioned his work, what he did?"

"No. They weren't very intimate conversations. But I liked him. He was very quiet but he seemed to have a lot to him—oh, I don't know, I guess you'd call it integrity."

"Well, there's lots of room for speculation. There must have been a reason why he didn't want you to know too much about his father. Anything else?"

"Yes. One very peculiar thing. Soon after his father died, he told me he was working on something that would put us on easy street for the rest of our lives. Of course, he was always talking schemes, so I didn't pay much attention."

"Right after his father died?"

"Yes."

"Must be a connection there. Anything else? Did he have any hobbies or talents?"

"Well, I don't know if you would say he was talented. I mean, he never made any money with his talents that I know of. But he always was sketching something, from landscapes to people. Mostly people. Some people who know, said his work was brilliant—his portrait work and some etchings he did before we were married. But he never tried to sell anything. He wouldn't even talk of it. He was very strange. But he was one of those rare people who could also build just about anything with his hands, from a chair to a motor. For a long time he went to night school, studying to be a machinist. But aside from puttering, he never put it to use."

"I'm not so sure about that. Maybe all his talents were used for what's in that box. Did he do any of that work around the house?"

"Oh, yes! He had a work shop, a kind of shed in the

back of the house. I was only in it a couple of times. But it was equipped with all kinds of lathes and gadgets I know nothing about. He used to spend hours on end out there. He kept it locked when he wasn't working there. Once I walked in when he was in the middle of something and he was furious. He said I might have spoiled a very delicate piece of work. I never went there again because it was right after that he installed a telephone so I could call him."

"Well," I said. "That tells us everything and nothing at the same time. Can you think of anything else?"

"No. Except that before he disappeared, he . . ."

"He disappeared!"

"Oh, yes. But I'll get to that. Before he disappeared, there were two or three men who used to visit him. He never brought them in the house, so I never met them. They always came to the workshop and always after dark. He told me they were gamblers and not people he wanted me to meet socially."

"I see. It all fits. But into what? Now tell me the rest, about his disappearance, the box, all of it."

"Well, one morning about six months ago, he went to work and he . . . he never came home. He just disappeared. I phoned his office and they said he left at the usual time and hadn't mentioned that he was going anywhere. I waited a few days because I thought he was on one of his gambling jaunts or whatever he did when he was away. But when he didn't show up in a week, I went to the Missing Persons Bureau. They tried, of course, but they couldn't find a trace of him.

"Then, about a month later, when I had given up in despair, I got a note from him. It had a Miami postmark. He said that he was sorry for all he had done to hurt me and that if I could be patient just a little longer, he would be back for good and that we would never have to worry about money again. He was about to put over this deal he had told me about. However, he said, if anything happened to him, I was to contact his lawyer, Mr. James Schroeder, and it was arranged that he, Mr. Schroeder, would take care of me out of funds given him for that purpose. Aside from a few more personal lines, that was all."

"And then something did happen to him?"

"Yes. A few weeks later I got a call from the Miami police. They had found George—his . . . his body, I mean, washed up on the beach. Aside from bruises that might have been caused by floating objects in the water, there wasn't a mark on him. Everything seemed to indicate that he had gone swimming and drowned. The strange part about it was that he was in his underwear, his shorts, and not a bathing suit. Their investigation turned up exactly nothing—not even where he was staying at the time. They figure he got out too far and just couldn't make it back.

"But they had no way to explain why his wallet was strapped to him in some kind of homemade waterproof pouch. It contained a couple of hundred dollars and some papers that led to me. And there it ended, except that I had to . . . to identify the body and arrange for burial. That part is too gruesome to even think about again and it has no bearing."

"I've been through it," I said. "Unfortunately, I can imagine the rest."

"Yes. Well, after . . . after it was over, a couple of weeks later, I went to this Mr. Schroeder, this lawyer. George had mentioned in his note that he could be trusted and that actually he was an outsider, in that he knew nothing about George's activities. I had to show Mr. Schroeder papers proving that George was dead. Even then, he called Miami. Then he produced a will in which George left everything to me. Everything was a safety deposit box containing a long letter and twenty-five thousand dollars in cash. I was shocked because

I had no idea he had that kind of money. And the letter was a greater shock.

"The letter contained instructions on where to find the box and what to do with it, its value and so on. You removed a section of plaster ceiling in one of our closets and it was in a space up there. I had to do it myself. It came away easily, but to look at it you would never know."

"What else did he say in the letter?"

"It's quite involved, so maybe I'd better show it to you." She went into the bedroom and brought back a long white envelope and handed it to me. I removed the typewritten sheets. The letter was long. It read:

Alicia, Dearest Angel,

Don't be sad. I was never much but a problem to you. You're free now, honey. And so am I. Of myself. I've always drifted toward trouble. And now I've found it. Or, since you're reading this, the end of it. There is some urge in me that would rather gamble or scheme up some way to beat the system of making it the hard way—like Joe Drudge.

I think it's more than that, too. I can't conform. The boredom would drive me insane. I crave excitement and can't find it any other way. Better a negative excitement than a positive boredom. That doesn't tell you much, but I'm not a psychologist and there are things about myself I don't understand. The important thing is that I have always loved you and that you should be taken care of after I'm gone. I've arranged everything and I want you to read these instructions very carefully.

There is twenty-five thousand dollars in a safety deposit box. How I got it is unimportant. I didn't steal it. It's yours. Schroeder will see that it's turned over to you. I had a special use for it that won't matter now.

Twenty-five thousand is a lot of money but it won't carry you but a small part of your life. I want you to be set as long as you live and there is a way.

This thing I told you I was working on is completed. If I were alive to put it in operation it would be worth millions to us. But I have someone else to take over and he will give you two hundred thousand cash.

Go to the closet in our bedroom. Remove the plaster from the ceiling—far right hand corner. You'll find a hammer and other tools in the kitchen, bottom drawer, left. Remember? Take the step ladder from the cellar. Even a chair will do. You won't have to remove more than a couple of square feet. The space above is hollow except for a cross beam. Chip the plaster around the beam until you can see a square, metal box. And don't make work of it. The plaster will come away easily once you get started. Under no circumstances are you to have anyone, man, woman or child, over to help you. You won't need any help and no one is to know about the box.

The box is quite heavy but not so as to be a problem to you. Find the carrying handle on top and lift it down gently. Don't drop the box or jar it unnecessarily. It will stand ordinary abuse, even a moderate fall. But a very severe blow might be dangerous. A puncture through the walls (an almost impossible task without special tools) would be fatal.

The box CANNOT be opened without keys and the combinations which you won't have, except in part. Don't try to *force* the box open or ask anyone else to do so. The box is rigged in such a way that it will explode, killing anyone near it, if it is forced open.

Now listen, Alicia. You know that I have never lied to you. This is the God's honest truth. That box cannot be tampered with! It would cost you your life. And the mechanism is so arranged that I doubt if even an expert on infernal machines (as they are called) could open it without detonating it.

The box is also waterproof, proof against any lock genius or crook who has sensitive fingers with a safe. I spent months thinking it out and designing it. Any attempt to beat the locks will destroy you, the clever boys and the contents. Don't try. Don't ask anyone else to. What the box contains must remain forever a secret from you.

This may sound like a foolish and dangerous thing that I have done. Perhaps. But I had to insure that you would not know what's in the box. For you to know would serve you no purpose at all on the one hand. And on the other, the knowledge would be extremely dangerous to you. Also, the value of the box depends upon keeping what it holds a secret. You would not be able to collect the two hundred thousand if you knew. Rigging the box so it couldn't be opened, even by my own wife, was part of the deal I made with Ralph Emory, about whom, more in a moment. He was not willing to pay the two hundred thousand without this insurance against the box being opened. So don't risk your life or anyone else's. Your only concern or interest is the money.

Ralph Emory, who lives just off Biscayne Boulevard in Miami, Florida, will pay over the money to you. You'll find his number in the Miami phone book under Ralph D. Emory. He is absolutely to be trusted. I've known him for years. Don't make any deals or contacts concerning the box with anyone else. Don't even give any important information to his wife if she answers when you call.

Emory is a big hunk of man. Over six feet. He must be in his mid-forties. He looks rugged. His manner may be a little frightening at times. Don't be deceived. He's intelligent, educated, even polished underneath. And he's honest! In *his* way. Especially insofar as anything that concerns me or mine, including this deal. He's a shrewd operator and he's made a fast buck all his life, sometimes just this side of the law, sometimes just the other side. But he has his own brand of ethics. Trust him! He knows all about the box and the arrangement. Get the money from him. Then clear out and forget you ever heard of him or the box. Don't meddle! Have a happy life. And a long one!

Taped to the bottom of the box you will find an envelope containing one key and the torn half of a hundred dollar bill. Also a code that will be meaningless to you. Don't try to solve it. You can't. Ralph will show you the matching half of the hundred and the other key. His key will match in size but will not be a duplicate. Your key opens one lock to the box, his the other. His half of the code together with yours will work the combinations of the inner box. Don't ask him to open it for you. He won't.

Now, I would not be writing this letter if I did not have reason to suppose my life is in danger. I have been followed and watched constantly. There are people who would torture or kill me to get that box. The box could be worth millions to the right person or persons. It is probably the most valuable thing of its kind in the world today. If I could be tortured or murdered for it, so could you. I have no reason to believe that *you* are being watched. But don't take a chance. You'll find my .45 pistol next to the box. Keep it around until the deal is closed. You know how to use it. I showed you once on a picnic in the woods. Remember? It's a pretty big weapon for a little girl. But it's all I have. Don't get trigger-happy. But use it if you must.

Emory can't come to you because he is also being watched. Don't ask me how anyone got wind of this thing because I don't know. You must take the box to Emory. Put it in my small black case. It just fits. At night, the later the better, sneak it out to the car and lock it in the trunk. The following day, drive to work as usual. Take no bags or clothing with you—nothing that would indicate a trip. Look up Brandon Charter Plane Service in the phone book. Ask for Lee Brandon. He's a friend, also to be trusted. He knows nothing about the box. Tell him nothing. He knows only that you may be taking a secret trip. He'll tell you how to get to the field. Better arrange this a day or so in advance. He might be chartered.

During your lunch hour (you can send a letter of resignation later if you like) drive to the airport. Don't tell Lee where you're going until you're in the air. He understands this. Just an extra precaution. Then have him fly you to Miami. When you get there, call Emory and he'll take over. Take nothing with you but the box. You can buy clothes later. All this is to safeguard against anyone knowing where you are going or that you are going at all.

One more thing. If, for some reason I can't imagine, Emory is unable to buy the box, don't try to sell it yourself. How could you anyway? You don't know what you're selling. Let Emory handle it. He has a kind of partner or associate who would buy it. Stay out of it. Let Emory handle it!

As I am very much alive now, it is a difficult thing to write as though I were dead. But I'm going to try.

News of my death will reach you somehow. If I'm missing for a certain time, Schroeder will instigate a hunt for me. He will know where to look but not why. Tell him nothing. Keep this letter secret. All right. So eventually you have proof that I am dead. And you may be told that I was murdered. All evidence may point to it. So what? I lived dangerously and I took my chances. I'm not sorry. Leave it alone. Don't try to find out how I was murdered or why. Leave it alone. Nothing you can do will bring me back. But almost anything you would do in trying to find out would put you in terrible danger of losing your own life. You wouldn't be playing a child's game against amateurs. You'd be committing suicide from the start. Leave it alone, baby. Please! Take the money and run. Stay out of Miami. Stay out of Florida. Stay out of trouble. It's all way over your head. Trust me. Obey!

This isn't exactly a sweet little farewell note. I had to put it the way I did. I wouldn't involve you even to this extent if there were any other way to get you the money. But I want you to have what I couldn't give you. You'll never have to worry about money again. Invest it carefully and live on the interest. I taught you all I know about investments. Emory will help there, too.

I am tempted now to get maudlin. I'll spare you. And myself. I'll sign off quickly. I'm sorry to have led you such a life. I have no excuse. I am what I am—or was what I was. Forgive me. I have never stopped loving you. I never will. God knows it. There's never been anyone else in my life. I can't tell you on paper what I've told you when you were next to me in the night. Add all those things to this letter and remember. So long, angel. Have a good life and a happy one. I've given you all I have. But be careful. It's a big piece of cake. But the knife cuts both ways . . .

Forever with love,
George

I gave her back the letter. "Well," I said. "This takes the cake for the strangest letter I ever read in my life. Doesn't sound like a bad guy—but plenty mixed up. What were your financial arrangements with Emory?"

"He had a check for two hundred thousand on a Ft. Lauderdale bank. He had deposited the money earlier and had the check with him. It was made out to me. We went into the bank and had my signature placed on a card for identification, so that when I signed it, I would have no trouble opening an account with it. It would be just like cash. For my benefit, he had the bank manager verify that the check was valid. When the box had been turned over to him with the keys and the code, we were to drive to his house where he would open it —in private, of course. Then if it contained what it was supposed to, he would give me the check."

"But at the time he was shot, you had the keys and the code in your possession."

"Yes."

"Of course anything could have happened. He could have opened it and claimed there was nothing but a couple of hunks of iron in it, kept the real contents and given the box back to you."

"That's true. But I had George's word that Emory was to be trusted—and George wasn't one to take chances. Not that kind of chance. Besides, I had a feeling that while Emory might be mixed up in God knows what, he had a certain kind of honor and loyalty."

"Honor among thieves."

"Is that supposed to include me and George?" she said sharply.

"I didn't mean it that way. But how do you know George wasn't mixed up in something crooked?"

"Because . . . well, I'm ashamed to say this. But after he died, I checked on him. He had no police record whatsoever."

"Then you did suspect?' '

"It was the box, I guess. If he had had a record, I might have assumed that what was in the box was stolen or illegitimate in some way. My conscience, you know. Aside from his gambling, I never knew him to be mixed up in anything at all."

"Yes, but with the kind of people running after the box willing to commit murder, wouldn't you assume it doesn't exactly smell too good?"

"Not necessarily. You can look at it another way. A lot of perfectly legitimate treasure has attracted crooks and always will. It could be and probably is, some invention of his that good as well as bad people would like to get their hands on."

"All right. If what the box contains is perfectly honest and legitimate, why couldn't it be turned over to the police. Let them open it and then you take whatever it contains and sell it to the highest bidder. The letter would prove ownership."

"That's a hard one to answer. But I'll try. In the first place, George's instructions were not to let it get into the hands of anyone but Emory. Besides, they wouldn't be able to open it and even if they could, there might be a legal battle of some kind and I might never get it back. And what's in the box is so valuable, even the police might take it for their own use."

"Ridiculous!"

"Is it? What about the Greenleaf kidnapping case in which thousands of dollars in the hands of detectives disappeared. And there are others."

"Well, I suppose it *could* happen, though it's unlikely."

"There again, I don't know. And I don't want to take any chances."

"Because you want the money."

"Yes. Oh, Burt, yes! If you'd lived in the state of semi-poverty I have, you'd understand what nearly a quarter of a million could mean. Freedom. Complete freedom from pinching through life. Freedom to travel. Freedom to have nice things—and I have expensive tastes. Is that a sin? Freedom to choose the kind of life you want to live and where you want to live it instead of being dictated to by circumstances."

"Well. What about the twenty-five thousand?"

"Fine. Very good. As far as it goes. But it could go just a couple of years and then you're back in the struggling department. Two hundred thousand is another matter. Why just the interest . . ."

"You mean one hundred eighty thousand. Don't forget my ten per cent."

"Unh-huh! You see. Money doesn't exactly scare *you* away either."

"Of course not. A month ago a million wouldn't have excited me but I'm regaining a little perspective. Just a little. I understand about the money. I just wanted to see if you'd looked at all the angles. One more thing. If this transaction is honest, why wouldn't George have let you make the sale on the open market to interested buyers?"

"I can only guess that perhaps he thought I would be cheated and that like, let's say certain art treasures, there is only a small interested market. Or if it's an invention, you would have patent rights to consider, all kinds of legal tangles. Secrecy would be a must. Also, this thing might be used for good purposes in some hands and bad in others. I just don't know."

"In any case, I guess you realize it's a dangerous situation. Until you get rid of that box, you're risking your life with it."

"And now yours. That's worse."

"Regardless, I've become involved and there's no way out. I won't run and it might not do any good with these people. They're too determined. Now. How do you intend to sell the box without Emory?"

"Well, his wife could probably put us in touch with this associate George mentioned."

"You don't know what he did for a living? Emory?"

"No. But obviously he was successful at it. He had money."

"All right. You have the address. So I'll make a little call on his wife and see what she knows. My God! I'll also have to decide what to tell her about him. I'll sleep on it. And we'll have to get rid of that box while I study possible ways to open it. The worst thing is to have it around here. Dangerous. I'll sleep on that, too. It's waterproof, isn't it?"

"George says so in his letter."

"Mmmmm. A good place for a waterproof box might be . . . I'll think about it. Be all right here for tonight. If they knew where it was they'd have been jolly well on the scene a long time ago."

"Oh, Burt! I don't know how I'd go on without you. And . . . and I want you to understand that while I do want the money, there's a much bigger reason why I don't drop the whole thing or turn it over to the police right now."

"What's that?"

"I made myself a promise, regardless of what he said in the letter, that I would do all I could to find out why George was killed and especially who killed him. Because I think he was murdered. And now Emory, too. And the only chance I have to find out is through that box. The police can't help. They wouldn't be able to open it. But Emory didn't have the code with him, so it must be in his house. If we can look in that box, we'll know most of the answers. Then we can turn it over to the police."

"Now you're talking. That's a motive I could like you for. And I'll help. But remember, one purpose might defeat the other. You find out what's in the box and you might not want to have anything to do with the sale of it. And there goes the money."

She smiled. "And your ten per cent."

"I'll risk it."

"And so will I. I may not have been what they call *in* love with George, but I always loved him and in his way he was good to me. So I owe him this much."

"What did Emory say about your husband's death?"

"He said he was terribly sorry, that in a way they were partners. He said he thinks he was murdered. And he was going to help me find out who did it. He said he was quietly investigating and he had some clues but nothing definite. That's all he would tell me."

"He's not going to help now," I said. "Let's have one for the road and call it a night."

I mixed a drink and sat down beside her on the couch. "I admit I had a few doubts about you," I said. "But they're vanishing." She smiled sadly and looked up at me so trustingly that I gave her a long kiss. I reached over and snapped out the table lamp, leaving a single light in the room. The kiss had started out to be tender but had prolonged into excitement. I had a sudden memory of her body startlingly exposed and vulnerable the night before. And, for the first time, I was relaxed enough to want her again.

As I kissed her I began to unfasten the buttons at the top of her dress. Half way down her hand closed on mine, gently but firmly.

"That's another thing I meant to talk to you about," she murmured. "Don't think I don't want you. But last night was a kind of drunken escape. I was in a frenzy and so tired of being scared. Next time we sleep together, let's mean it. At least, let's not be escaping from anything. I'm no prude—far from it. But believe me, there hasn't been anyone since George."

She redid the buttons while I redid my estimate of her. Then I asked her, "Just what was it that you were escaping from? If no one knew where you were, why did you have to hole up in your apartment?"

"That's the part I haven't told you about," she said.

"I followed the instructions George gave me. I was very careful. I chartered a plane from Brandon on the condition I wouldn't have to give my destination until we were in the air. It cost me plenty. In Miami I rented a car, not knowing where to go. I was just riding around town trying to think it out, when I looked in my mirror and . . . and I saw that same big, dark sedan, a Buick, I think, the one that stopped us when I was with Emory, following me. I couldn't lose it—especially in broad daylight.

"Finally I drove it into one of those quick-wash places. There was a line around back of this wash rack that looks like it's under a big quonset hut. I was out of sight. While I was waiting, I purposely got talking to a decent-looking woman behind me. I told her a man, a masher type, was following me and I had to lose him. She was very understanding. She let me transfer my baggage to her trunk. Then I drove my car up to the rack at the point where they take it from you. When my car was done, the attendant drove it outside and parked it. I had told him I would come back for it, that I wanted to do some shopping. Then, while we were still inside the building, I slipped into this woman's car and crouched on the floor in back and we drove away. Later I phoned the car rental place and told them where to pick it up. The deposit was more than enough, so I just let them keep it.

"The woman told me about Ft. Lauderdale, so I took a taxi there and found this place. Later, I bought the Cadillac. It was a silly luxury, but I've wanted one all my life. This one was slightly used and I got a good bargain. I stayed hidden because I knew there was a chance I would be spotted."

"Why didn't you call Emory right away?"

"I did. Some woman answered and said he was in Europe and she didn't know exactly when he would be back. She asked a lot of questions but I didn't tell her anything but where I could be reached. I didn't even give my real name. I gave the name Shafton."

"So that's why you were waiting around here. He was in Europe. What do you think he was doing there?"

"I asked him. He said it had something to do with preparation for using what's in the box. But when he heard George was dead, he flew right back."

"My God! Sounds like this thing has world-wide implications. But I see now why you were scared. God in heaven, where do these thugs get their information? The same damn Buick. It scares hell out of me, too. Let's get some sleep."

"Burt?"

"Yes?"

"One other thing. A confession. I phoned your office in Buffalo to check on you. I just couldn't take a chance —on anyone."

"I know all about it," I said. "I got a call from the office and when they told me some gal was asking questions, I checked with long distance and found it was you."

She smiled. "You're a sly one."

"I don't take chances either. And while we're confessing, I followed you and Emory to Ft. Lauderdale. I lost you after you came out of the bank . . ."

"Burt! You don't trust me."

"I didn't. I may yet, though," I said smiling.

She took a roll of bills from her purse and handed them to me. "Here's the other five hundred . . . I don't expect you to trust me. But this may help."

"I trust you enough that I feel a little guilty taking your money," I said.

"Don't. You more than earned it." She stretched, got up and went to the door.

"Speaking of trust," I said. "Wouldn't you rather take the box with you?"

"No thanks," she said. "I don't think you'll be trying to open it. It's all yours for the night. And Burt. Sleep tight."

CHAPTER EIGHT

I HAD A LATE BREAKFAST with Alicia in the morning. She invited me over to her place and I brought the black case with its box along. After we finished eating, I lighted a cigarette and studied her across the table. It was extremely warm and she wore nothing but a yellow halter and shorts to match. As usual, she managed to look languidly sensual and at the same time crisp and alert. I found myself wishing there was nothing to separate us from the pure pursuit of sunny pleasure and finding each other out. And yet in the back of my mind there was always the lumpy sadness of the need for Bev, and the urgent, dangerous necessity of dealing with this thing of the box.

"How would you like to go fishing?" I said. "With maybe a little swimming thrown in?"

She had been sitting pensive and silent and her face suddenly brightened. "Wonderful!" she said. "I'd love it." The joy drained away from her face as suddenly as the eagerness had come to it—like a child who remembers that it's a school day. "Huh," she said disgustedly. "For a minute I thought you really meant it."

"I did."

"You know we haven't time to play like vacation. Besides there's always the danger of being . . ."

"We'll have to risk it. Because this combines business with pleasure. In fact, the pleasure is only a cover for the business."

"I don't get it."

"You will. This is a game called hide the box. Got a bathing suit?"

She nodded.

"Climb into it then. I've got mine on underneath my clothes. I have a little shopping to do and by the time it's done, we'll be ready for a dip."

"Okay," she said. "Have you thought it out carefully?"

"It kept me awake quite awhile last night."

"I didn't need anything extra to keep me awake," she said, and disappeared in the bedroom. She was back in a minute wearing a bathing suit, a beach robe and sandals. I opened the black case and removed the steel box. "I'll need a blanket," I said.

When she brought it, I wrapped the box inside it. "Now it won't look conspicuous," I told her. "Let's go."

We took her car because mine might be recognized and Cadillac convertibles are about as prominent as Fords in Southern Florida on the east coast. We stopped in town at one of those Army-Navy stores. I bought a sturdy waterproof case that might once have been used to protect some piece of signal corps equipment or demolition and an oilskin cover.

Next we stopped at a boat supply house where I bought a small boat anchor, and two lengths of rugged mooring chain to the ends of which were bolted large, galvanized spring snaps.

As Alicia drove back toward the beach, I wrapped the weird metal box in oil cloth, placed it in the waterproof case and bolted the lid securely. Using the big snaps, I fastened the two ends of the chains to carrying handles at either end of the box. The other end of one chain I attached to the anchor. Again I used the blanket for concealment.

"Simple. One end of the box is chained to an anchor, the other to a dock piling. If it gets loose from the dock, the anchor still holds it. The damn thing is so heavy it probably wouldn't move far if it wasn't chained at all."

"Where's this dock?"

"You'll see."

Ft. Lauderdale has a network of inland waterways or canals. They are everywhere. And houses of assorted sizes, some downright palatial, skirt their banks. Many of the houses boast docks for anything from rowboats to immense yachts. There are so many of these waterways that the town is often called "The Venice of America."

Watching to see that we weren't followed, I guided Alicia along one of these waterways that I had investigated some time before I knew the knowledge of it would come in handy. It was a back street a few blocks from where we lived. I told her to stop when we came to a large, vacant lot. I had once walked across this lot to the water's edge. It was then that I had noticed that someone had built a sturdy little dock for small boats. This, perhaps in preparation for a house that for some reason was never begun. In any case, the dock wasn't being used now and the nearest houses were at some distance, screened from us by tall palms and vegetation.

Carrying the blanket with the notorious box in the watertight case, we moved across the lot. Alicia carried my fishing rod and one of these water-tight masks I had once used for skin diving. If anyone had seen us, we might have appeared like a carefree couple with fishing gear and picnic supplies.

We sat for a long time on the dock, pretending to fish. Actually, we were watching carefully in every direction. Boats cruised past in the canal, but otherwise, there appeared to be no one. We sat above one of the pilings at the end of the dock and, after awhile, I cautiously held the blanket near the edge and allowed the case, anchor and all to fall into the water with a minimum splash. There is little current in these canals. The water is always pretty calm. So I wasn't worried about the gear moving from where it lay at the bottom next to the piling.

Next we made a great pretext of swimming and playing in the water, diving and splashing. It was all unnecessary. There wasn't a soul around. Once, as we treaded water, Alicia asked, "Why do we need a waterproof case if the box itself is waterproof?"

"An extra precaution," I said. "Besides, the water might not help the locks any. And if the case isn't perfectly waterproof, I've got the box wrapped in oil skin."

"Let's get it over with, then," she said.

I pulled the mask over my eyes and dove under the water, following the piling down. The water was clear and not so deep that I couldn't see. It was about fourteen feet to the bottom. By working and then surfacing, then submerging again, I had the whole job done in ten minutes. I looped one end of the chain around the piling and closed the loop with the snap. Then I extended the anchor so that the case rode in the center, secured at either end. It was awkward work under water, but not difficult. You didn't really have to see and I wished I had tried it with the increased safety of night.

"Well," I said to Alicia, "that'll hold it. Now let's not rush away. We'll pretend we're having fun."

"I almost am," she said. So we stayed for a couple of hours, sunning and swimming and also watching. Then we went home.

We were back in her apartment a little after three, sipping Manhattans. Alicia seemed more relaxed. "I feel better," she said. "Not having that thing around. I still don't understand quite how you did it. The case is chained to the piling?"

"Yes. It has a very strong, metal carrying handle at either end. The chains clamp the handles and fasten to the anchor and the piling. If, for some reason, the chain breaks away from the piling, the anchor will still hold the case. They're fastened independently."

"It seems foolproof. You don't think anyone saw us?"

"I'm positive. Unless they were watching through field glasses from a great distance. Even so, unless they were our friends of the Buick, watching would be accidental and wouldn't tell them much. If we were watched by people who know, which I seriously doubt, we're sunk anyway. I mean, if they know where we are, it's all over but the shouting."

"You mean shooting, don't you?" she said bitterly.

"Not necessarily. These characters are clever enough not to risk any killing without purpose. What they want is that box, not some kind of revenge because we have it. I think they would make every effort to get it without killing."

"Maybe just a little quiet bludgeoning," she said. "With some rare forms of torture thrown in."

I smiled. "I hope we aren't ever in the way of finding out. Unlike movie heroes, I'm inclined to wax talkative when lighted cigarettes are applied to the soles of my feet or when I feel the bones snapping in my arms."

"All they'd have to do is tickle the soles of my feet," she said. "What do we do now?"

I looked at my watch. "As your agent, ten percent gives me that title, you know, perhaps I should make a call at Emory's house."

"Are you sure you want to get into that now?"

"I'm not sure of anything except that I'm under a compulsion to keep moving. During the war, the hardest part was the waiting, not always the fighting. And when I wait I think—usually about the wrong things. Anyway, we have no other clue."

"All right," she said wearily. "Dear God, but I'll be glad when this is over. I'll get the address for you."

"While you do that, I'm going to change my clothes. Be right back."

When I returned, Alicia gave me the keys to the Cadillac and an address in Miami. "Try not to be very long this time," she said. "I go crazy. Do you want the gun—the .45?"

"I'm going to leave it with you," I said. "You won't need it, but it'll do more for your nerves than an aspirin."

"I don't think you should go anywhere unarmed."

"Emory's widow, poor woman, shouldn't give me any trouble."

She kissed me lightly. "Hurry back, then."

I left.

Emory's house was a long, low and rambling structure a few blocks off Biscayne Boulevard and right on Biscayne Bay. It was of a type known as Polynesian modern and was probably thrown together for around a hundred thousand. I had little trouble finding it and I was pretty certain I wasn't followed along the way.

The door was opened by an attractive maid in a starched and filigreed white apron. She was young and looked not too recently removed from the island of Cuba, though her English was as spotless as her apron.

"My name is Keating," I opened. "And I'd like to see Mrs. Emory on a personal matter."

The girl's face admitted that there was a Mrs. Emory and didn't deny my right to see her. With a small smile and a nod of her head, she ushered me in. I was a little surprised that anything connected with the whole dirty business could be painless.

I was left to wait in a large, sunken oval of a living room with massive, modern furniture and situated along the side of the house facing the bay. The maid tiptoed away and left me in an air-conditioned silence so profound it was distracting.

I had time to study the salt water furrowing of a launch across the picture window vista, create my own images from the design of a lone cumulus cloud in the azure distance and light a cigarette, when I felt the approach of someone over the ankle-deep fluff of white carpet.

Mrs. Emory wasn't quite what I expected. She was, if anything, younger than her maid and just as dark, though her darkness was not Cuban but Florida sun. Her hair was also dark and medium long. Her eyes were ripe olive black with an enamel luster and something of enamel's hardness. That is, if eyes can be hard and male-loving at the same time. She managed it.

She was short, almost tiny, but amazingly buxom for her size. The almost perfect oval of her face lost softness in the sharp little point of her chin, the somewhat pouty droop of heavy lips. But I'm taking her apart piece by piece for inspection and altogether she lacked nothing for male excitement. And she flowed into the room with the studied litheness of one who knows it.

She paused a few feet from me and toyed with a diamond-studded, gold bracelet. "Yes," she said. "I'm Mrs. Emory. What is it?" Her voice had the cool condescension and enthusiasm of a housewife for a door to door salesman. But I noticed that when I stood up, her eyes flicked over me appraisingly before they came back to my own.

"My name is Burt Keating, Mrs. Emory. I'm not selling anything, if that helps. But I don't know just where to start. You see really, I'm acting for someone else. A Mrs. McCabe. Alicia McCabe."

Her face changed slowly. There was recognition and interest. She became quite cordial. "Sit down," she said. "Would you like a drink? Scotch or bourbon?"

"Bourbon," I said. "On the rocks."

She reached beneath a table and pressed something and, in a moment, the Cuban girl reappeared. "Bourbon on the rocks and Scotch and soda, Manita," she said, looking not at the girl but at me.

"I take it you know of Mrs. McCabe," I said.

"I've heard Ralph, my husband, mention her often."

"Then I guess you also know that Alicia, Mrs. McCabe, was in the process of a business transaction with your husband?"

"Oh yes," she nodded. "I know about it. At least not the details, but . . . well, Ralph doesn't bring business home." She smiled as though at some secret joke.

The maid brought drinks on a tray and went away.

"The point is, Mrs. Emory, I'm sort of an agent for Mrs. McCabe and I want to complete that transaction. But if you don't know the details, I mean if you aren't prepared to handle it yourself, perhaps you can turn me over to someone who can. Some associate of your husband's."

"I don't see why," she said a little sharply. "Ralph can handle his own business."

"Then you don't know. I mean, well of course, you couldn't."

"Don't know what—Burt?"

There was a kind of insolent familiarity in her use of my first name. I ignored it. "You don't know about your husband? What—what happened?"

She laughed disparagingly. "I know everything about my husband. Of course! What could happen?"

There was something about her tone, her attitude that irked me so much I wanted to say, Your husband is dead —shot through the head. I restrained the impulse and searched for a new tack. "Let's put it this way. How long since you've seen your husband?"

"Ralph?" Her smile said I was an idiot. "About ten minutes ago."

"Ten minutes!"

The same smile. "Give or take a minute or two."

"Ten minutes? Ten minutes, you say!" She merely stared at me.

I was a long time rearranging the picture. "But I thought . . ."

"You thought what?"

"Nothing," I said. "I didn't know he was here. May I see him then?"

She stood up. "Certainly," she said. "You should have asked for him in the first place."

I started to open my mouth, but she said, "On the other hand—Burt—I'm glad you said hello to me first. Very thoughtful." She turned around and walked briskly across the room, her high, firm buttocks waving an insolent goodbye.

She disappeared around a corner and then leaned back into the room. "By the way," she called, "my name is Millicent. Millie is all right. And Ralph is away more than he's here. I get lonely. So, come back again. Any time—Burt. Bring that Mrs. what's-her-name—McCabe. That is, if you like." She was gone with a quick neon flash of white teeth in the sun-dark face.

I sat there waiting for Ralph Emory. And I swear to God, no one ever waited with more curiosity.

CHAPTER NINE

THE MAN who came into the room was not Ralph Emory. At least he did not resemble the man Alicia had called Emory. He was somewhat older, not quite as tall, but at the same time altogether a much bigger man. He was one of those people you think of as heavy or beefy, rather than fat. Perhaps it is the bone structure. Some people are just built to carry a lot of weight. So much flesh on a lesser frame would have been ridiculous. This one had the look of a heavyweight whose prowess in the ring was only a distant memory, while much of the animality and power remained just beneath the loose flesh of softer years.

And again, there is the distribution of weight that takes away the impression of fatness. This man began to be big at the grey-brown dome of his great skull and never stopped. His broad forehead, Roman nose, wide, loose mouth and rock-hewn jaw were leonine. Even his neck looked thick beyond strangling, his shoulders immense, the rest of him—arms, hands, thighs to feet, out-sized. I was surprised, therefore, when he moved toward me over the carpet with easy grace and, when he spoke, his voice was so deeply soft as to be almost inaudible.

"What can I do for you?" he said politely. "I'm Ralph Emory."

He had one great mitt extended toward me but, for a moment, I was unable to take it. "You are Ralph Emory?" I said stupidly.

He didn't answer me. He continued to hold out his hand and regard me calmly from unblinking brown eyes.

Finally I took his hand and shook it hesitantly. His grasp was firm without trying to be. There was something in his manner that was too overpowering for mere random questions, so I simply said, "I'm Burt Keating. Glad to know you."

"We can talk in the den," he said.

I followed him out of the living room, across a hall and into a square, oak-paneled room containing a large, kidney-shaped desk, red leather chairs and a small bar. There were also several shelves of books which looked well read, not merely ornamental. Jalousied windows captured a diagonal view of the bay. I sat down in a chair opposite the desk.

"Drink?" he said.

"Bourbon and soda."

He had already turned the great mass of his back to me and was busy with bottles on a shelf behind the bar. His movements were slow and careful and some aura about him seemed to forbid conversation. I remained silent. He held the drink out to me in passing and took his own to the desk where he laid it on a coaster. The polished surface of the desk was bare except for pen and holder and telephone.

Ignoring his drink, he settled into the big, high-backed chair, built a pyramid with his fingers and waited with the same placid face for me to speak. And for a long moment, I couldn't think of a single opening. I decided to be direct.

"I was sent here as a kind of agent for Mrs. Alicia McCabe," I began. His expression didn't change. "I'm slightly puzzled, to put it mildly. Because day before yesterday, Mrs. McCabe was in contact with a man who claimed to be Ralph Emory. I met this man myself. And I can't say you bear much resemblance to him— Mr. uh . . . Emory."

He picked up his drink, took a swallow and considered me over the rim of the glass. "What is this business you want to conduct for Mrs. McCabe?"

"I'm not prepared to tell you until I understand what happened to the man who represented himself as Ralph Emory. But I will tell you it concerns a valuable possession that came to Alicia McCabe when her husband died. She's prepared to sell it to the right person—when we find out who that person is. It's a little confusing."

"And how is it that she hasn't come herself?"

"Because she thought you . . . uh . . . Mr. Emory was dead."

A slight smile crossed his face. "As you see, any report that I'm dead has been slightly exaggerated. Are you a relative of Mrs. McCabe?"

"A friend."

"And your business?"

"Well, not that it's important, but I manage a loan company in Buffalo. I'm on leave of absence."

"Have you any papers to prove it?"

"Why should I prove it?"

"Because if you don't, you'd better finish your drink and get out. Do you think I do business with any stranger that rings my doorbell?"

"I guess that's reasonable." I showed him an employee's identification card and my New York State driver's license. He looked at them briefly and compared the signatures. He took a piece of paper from a drawer and handed me the desk pen. "Write your name on this, please." I wrote it and again he compared signatures. He handed back the license and identification card.

"This will be easy to check," he said. "But you seem all right." For the first time he really smiled—not a warm smile, of which he probably wasn't capable—but his lips widened across his face. "I'm sorry," he said. "But if you know anything about this thing, you know we have to be careful." He paused. "Now. The man posing as me was a private investigator whom I hired for the purpose."

He let that sink in a moment and for the first time I felt some relief and a little understanding. Sitting there, overflowing the chair, he was as McCabe said in his letter—a big hunk of man. And very formidable.

"I brought this man in from the middle West for the simple reason that his face isn't known here," he went on. "Also because he knows his business. I've used him before. You see, there are certain people in this area who have such an unfriendly rivalry in the acquisition of this possession of Mrs. McCabe's, they might just kill me. They are more watchful that you can imagine and it seemed uh . . . wise, to send someone else."

"Of course you haven't heard from this man? This investigator?"

"Nothing. He just vanished. However, I take it he didn't have the uh . . . box with him."

"No. Alicia—I can't seem to call her Mrs. McCabe—Alicia told me that the man was shot and killed on the truck route to Miami from Ft. Lauderdale. Alicia was with him when they were held up and he was taken from the car and shot resisting. She got away."

"Terrible! And the box?"

"She hadn't delivered it to him yet."

"Good. That much is good."

"What are you going to do about the detective or investigator, or whatever you call him? Police?"

"Perhaps. Eventually, of course. Right now there isn't any evidence except uh . . . Alicia's word. We might be able to find out more under cover. I have ways. Now. However cold-blooded it may seem to disregard the investigator for the time being, we can't help him now, so let's get down to business. Where is the box at the moment?"

"I don't know," I lied. I didn't think it was any of his business regardless of how trustworthy George McCabe had thought him to be.

"You don't know!"

"Alicia knows. She can get it when the time comes."

He nodded. "Well, it doesn't matter. You'll bring it here? Or send Alicia with it?"

"That depends. What about the money? The investigator had your check, didn't he?"

"I've already had it stopped at the bank. In any case, I doubt if a check for such a large amount could be cashed or deposited without all the identification in the world."

"Probably so. But you're prepared to pay Alicia McCabe two hundred thousand as agreed?"

He studied his cigarette for a moment, rolling it between thumb and forefinger. "No," he said evenly. "I'm not. I was, but I'm not."

"Why?"

"There are many reasons. You see, Mr. Keating, my business is speculation. Mostly on the market. Occasionally I dabble in other things . . . I gamble on items that some people wouldn't touch. Sometimes it pays off, sometimes it doesn't. I've had large reverses—as late as yesterday. But principally, this thing has become too hot. Too much danger connected with handling it. In fact, your report that my investigator was killed, strengthens my point. Really, Mr. Keating, it's insanity for me to close this deal at all. But I'll do it—at my price."

"What's your price?"

"Fifty thousand."

"Fifty thousand! Why that's just a fraction. I thought you made a promise to George McCabe."

"Did you know George?"

Suddenly I decided on a plan. "Yes," I said. "He was one of my best friends."

"Then you know he was a dreamer. He was inclined to exaggerate, to put it kindly."

"Yes, but . . ."

"And though I did say his . . . his . . . the box might be worth two hundred thousand to me, I also said that it would depend on how guarded he was, how much he kept it secret. It's hardly a secret any longer with half a dozen gunmen shooting down everyone connected with it. I think he slipped there. And while we were close friends, even partners, and in a way I considered him a kind of genius, two hundred thousand is stretching friendship a bit under the circumstances. The whole value of this thing depends on secrecy. Obviously George talked somewhere and broke our agreement. For instance, do *you* know what's in the box?"

This was what I was waiting for. I made the stab and while I was at it, made a good one. "Well," I said thoughtfully, "for a moment I was tempted to lie to you, but—well, yes, I know."

I could see this really got to him because his eyes widened slightly, which was a large display of emotion for him. It was almost a minute before he spoke again, a muscle in his jaw working as though he was chewing it over. "Then you know about the jewels," he said, almost sadly.

The news knocked me out for a second but I recovered quickly. "Yes," I said. "I know about the jewels."

His big features became suddenly amused in a sardonic way. "You're a goddamn liar," he said softly. "There are no jewels in that box."

I forced a laugh. "Well, it was a good try."

"Not good enough, Keating. You don't have an idea in the world what's in that box. You couldn't have. It can't be opened. Fifty thousand. Take it or leave it. And let me advise you, you'd better take it. Your life and your girl friend's aren't worth a dirty cigar butt while you hold that box. You'd lose it anyway to these thugs. Now get out of here and call me when you're ready to do business." He swung his chair so that he was looking out upon the oblique view of the bay and I might as well have been alone. I left without a word and without being shown out.

On the way back I felt a return of the old, morbid depression. It always crept over me without warning, sneaking in like early morning fog blanketing the ocean and hiding the sun. The surprise conversation with Emory had gone none too well for Alicia. I thought I could outsmart him and I had bungled. That didn't help my mood. But of course Bev, or the loss of her, was always on the edge of my mind. And that was the real depression.

And then I came to an intersection and there was a bottleneck. Traffic moved slowly around a minor accident. Two cars had bounced off each other, one hitting the other broadside. There was the usual torn metal and fragments of glass strewn over the road. A small crowd had gathered around the two cars, which had a sad, beaten look, as though they might never run again. I couldn't see if anyone was hurt for the crowd. I moved away, out of sight. But the image lingered.

The wreck in which Bev had been involved had been cleared away before I got the news. But I remembered the cruel impersonality of the picture in the morning paper, the flashbulb-white faces of the thrill-seekers staring, the car door flung half open, permitting a view of one dangling, twisted leg, the known, stockinged leg, once warm against mine in the night, revealed to the thigh, shoeless and grotesque for morbid watchers. "Mangled body of Mrs. Beverly Keating before it was pulled from wreckage on Greenhill Road."

I never could quite lose the picture. It came crawling into my mind with all its obscene detail, unwanted as a dirty black spider out of the woodwork. And with the sadness, came the doubts, the "ifs." If only I had gone in her place. If only I had said something to her as she went out the door, some kind little thing to take with her. If only we had been better stocked and there had been no need to go at all. If only she had left a minute later . . . One minute would have made all the difference—thirty seconds even, and she would have been past that crossroad. It was useless. It got me nowhere. It gave me a weeping sickness without tears.

And now the feeling slopped over into the present. There was at least this small clinging to Alicia. And I had the strange sensation that if I didn't hurry, hurry! she would be gone when I got back. I shoved down on the accelerator and flew dangerously at Ft. Lauderdale.

CHAPTER TEN

S HE WAS THERE ALL RIGHT. She came quickly to the door before the chime sound died away. "Don't look so startled," I said.

"Somehow I always worry," she said, and followed me into the room.

We fell into chairs and lighted cigarettes. "The last few miles I got kind of anxious myself. But it's always harder to wait than to be doing something."

"I know. I've just been sitting here chain smoking. Couldn't even read. You weren't followed?"

"No. I'm sure."

"Good. What's the news?"

"It's shocking. The guy with the other key and the torn hundred dollar bill—did he say he was Ralph Emory?"

"Yes. Of course."

"Did he show you any identification, anything like that?"

"No, but he brought the key and . . . What are you driving at?"

"He wasn't Emory."

"I don't believe it."

"I just talked to Emory at his house."

"No! You couldn't have."

"The one you . . . the one that got killed was some sort of private investigator. Emory sent him because he was afraid he might be tailed."

"How weird! Give me all of it."

So I told her. She asked a lot of questions and then she said, "I suppose I should be relieved that he's alive and I have a buyer. But do you think I should accept fifty thousand? It's quite a comedown."

"I don't know," I told her. "Emory has a point, though. He has several. The box isn't worth near as much to him if the secret of it leaked out. Not knowing what's in it, I don't know exactly why. But I can imagine. In any case, he takes the risk of being gunned while holding it. And you take a greater risk without advantage of being able to use the contents."

"Why do I take a greater risk?"

"Because he probably knows who and what he's fighting and he has enough money and power and organization to protect himself. He's tough and shrewd and he has experience in these things. We're like babies playing with uncaged wildcats."

"You seem to have a little experience yourself."

"I have combat experience and this is a kind of war. I've been in some deadly situations and when the chips are down I can play rough, too. But I'm only one man and I don't even know what the fight's about. It's hard to deal with an enemy when you don't even know what motivates him."

"Too bad you couldn't have trapped Emory into telling what's in the box."

"Huh. Not that one. He's a slick article."

"Then you think I should take the fifty thousand?"

"As a last resort, of course you'll have to. But if we could find out what's in that box, you might be able to get your price or more."

"Is there any way at all?"

"I don't have the know-how to open it with any degree of safety. But . . ."

"But what?"

"Well . . . You still have those numbers, the code, don't you?"

"Yes."

"There might be a way to find the other part of it. Is there any significance to the torn hundred?"

"Probably. But aside from identification, I don't know."

"We've got to get the rest of that code," I said. "Emory would have it. He wouldn't even pay fifty thousand if he didn't."

"So where does that leave us?"

"Fifty thousand is still a lot of money."

"Whose side are you on?"

"Yours, of course. But we're working against impossible odds. And fifty thousand is . . ."

"A lot of money. I know. The difference is this. With fifty thousand, you're well off, but you're still living carefully. With two hundred thousand, well . . . Besides, once we give up the box, there's no clue to George and what happened to him."

"The clue to much of it will be inside that box. I've got to get that code."

"You don't think there's a way, do you?"

"A slim possibility."

"How?"

"Through Millicent Emory."

"No!"

"Yes. Maybe. She's vulnerable. Just how vulnerable, I don't know. She likes men but I don't think she cares a bean about her husband. He's not exactly the white collar ad type. He's got a big, animal's body and a subtle mind. I don't think she likes ugly animals and she's not too subtle. Or loyal."

"Then why would she be hooked up with Emory?"

"For gain. Although the way she acts, it doesn't look like he's bought her loyalty with money, either. Not yet, anyway. She may not have a sou of her own and independent loot might buy her." I didn't want to tell Alicia that a little masculine attention of the extra marital variety might persuade her, too.

"I take it you don't like Emory?" she said.

"I don't like him and I don't dislike him particularly. He's quite a boy. You can't help admiring some things about him. I imagine he'd be a good friend and a terrible enemy. I think he intended to stick to his original agreement with your husband. But circumstances change and maybe George did talk somewhere. About what? It's all so ridiculous not knowing."

"And what about Mrs. Emory?"

"I'd trust her like a full grown crocodile around the house. But for our purposes she might be useful."

"You think you could get the code through her?"

"I might with the right offer of a cut. Or if I could just get a little time to snoop around the house."

"Is it ethical?"

"To find out what's in the box? It belongs to you, doesn't it? One way or another, your husband got killed over it, didn't he? And the detective, too. Ethics don't hold when you're trying to uncover a reason for murder."

"Maybe she could simply tell you what's in the box."

"If she knows. And she might. She just might."

"How would you get in touch with her?"

"Go and see her."

"With Emory there?"

"With Emory out."

"When would that be?"

"She says he's out most of the time. We could call and check."

"When?"

"Now."

"You wouldn't go back there tonight!"

"I'd hate to. But I have a feeling our time is running out on this thing. If not tonight, tomorrow. And tomorrow may be too late."

"You're always leaving me."

"I'll give up on this thing if you like. It wouldn't take much persuasion. We could get out of here and run over to the West coast—Tampa—some place like that. Let the box cool under water. It might not solve anything, but really, Alicia, you'd be better off. A lot safer."

"Do you care?"

"Of course I care. Don't go feminine on me, now."

"I . . . I . . ." She looked like she was going to cry.

"I'm sorry," I said. "I'm pretty drum-tight. One part of me doesn't care what happens and another part of me that comes from knowing you, does care."

"All right," she said. "Let's make another try. Do you want me to call?"

"Yes. Give it a whirl."

"What if he's there?"

"Talk to him. Tell him you haven't got the box here but you could get your hands on it if he's willing to compromise—a hundred and twenty-five thousand. See what he says. Just stall him. If he's not there, the maid will probably answer the phone. Don't leave any message."

She got the number from her purse and placed the call. It was a short conversation. Emory wasn't in.

"Was that the maid?"

"Yes."

"When did she say he'd be back?"

"She said he wouldn't be back tonight. He left a number where he could be reached if it was important. She asked if I was Mrs. McCabe. I said no, and it wasn't important."

"Uh-huh. He was expecting your call. I'll bet he's anxious. More than fifty thousand worth if we knew what we were bargaining with."

"Are you going?"

"After dinner. Let's go out for a change."

"How do you know Millicent Emory will be there?"

"I don't. And I couldn't let you ask. I'll pretend I dropped in to see Emory. If she's there, she's there."

"Ugh," she said. "Let's eat."

We had dinner at the hotel nearby. We lingered quite awhile over it, agreeing not to spoil our enjoyment by any further discussion of the box. Alicia told me something about herself, among other things that her mother died when she was a baby, her father when she was nineteen. She was an only child and although her father had given her every advantage his small means would allow, she had never known a time when money wasn't a nagging worry. She had an aunt in New York and a cousin in Tacoma. She wasn't close to either. She sent them Christmas cards but never saw them. Essentially, she was alone.

After dinner and a couple of drinks, I was still reluctant to leave, so we walked for a half an hour or so along the water's edge, chatting arm in arm about nothing in particular. Finally I took her back to her apartment, and in the Cadillac set out again for Emory's. It was half past eight.

The little Cuban maid opened the door. Of course she said Ralph Emory wasn't at home. I didn't have to ask to see Mrs. Emory. She was standing in the background and I wasn't surprised when she invited me in.

"As long as you're here, you might as well have a drink," she said and sent the maid for the usual Scotch and bourbon.

She had the drinks served on the patio overlooking the water on the back side of the house. It was very pleasant. She wore what looked like satin lounging pajamas of pale green. From the way her breasts, even the nipples, threatened to burst through the material, it was quite obvious she wore nothing underneath. I don't suppose she had been expecting anyone, but in any case she didn't rush away to change. She did say that she had just climbed from the tub and I'd have to excuse her appearance. I was quite willing.

"Are you married, Burt?" It was the first question she

asked me after the drinks were served and she had told the maid if she needed anything more she'd get it herself. "Run along to your little man, Manita."

"No," I said. "I'm not married." And that's all I said. I wasn't going to go through the rest of it. Not for her.

It was quite dark on the patio, but not so dark that I didn't catch the quick, sly flash of her smile. She considered her drink a moment, stirring the ice with one finger. Then she said, "What made you come back so soon? Did Mrs. McCabe decide to sell her little box at Ralph's price?"

"Then you know about it?"

"Oh, yes. There are some things I make it my business to know. The things that interest me. Well . . .?"

"Let's put it this way—Mrs. McCabe wants to discuss a compromise."

In the semi-gloom, there was the arrogant shake of her head. "I think she's wasting her time. You don't compromise with Ralph in this kind of poker. Not unless you have an ace in the hole. And you don't, do you?"

"I might have a pat hand. But I'm not showing it just now."

"Huh! I doubt it. And if you're bluffing, he'll call you. Is she your girl friend?"

"She's a friend. Period."

"Period. And exclamation point. What's in it for you then? Everyone wants something." Again there was the secret smile. The remark was a real clue to her philosophy, if I needed one. I decided there was an advantage in at least pretending to talk her language.

"Sure. We all have our little price."

"I'll bet you come high."

"I manage. What do you know about the box? Know what's in it?"

"Listen. If I did know, and I'm not saying I do, I wouldn't tell you."

"Sure. Because you know what side of the bread has jam on it."

She laughed. A hard, brittle sound. "It's more like I know when to keep out of a jam. I wait and I watch. And I listen, too. Oh, Burty boy. Such a nice, clean-cut guy to be playing such games. Playing Russian roulette in the back room when you belong in front sipping sloe gin with pink ladies. Ha, haaaa."

"Does that mean you think I'm too soft to mix in this league? Don't underestimate. Remember what Uncle Teddy said, 'Speak softly and carry a big stick.' "

"Oh, I don't underestimate. Not since Ralph. I used to underestimate him, you know. But everyone, and I mean everyone, has their weak spot—right where they live. Oh no, Burty boy, you're not soft. I'd bet money on it. And that's where I live—that's one of the places." She smiled, a slow creeping back of her lips. "But you'd be surprised if you knew the things you don't know. And listen, I like you and I . . . Never mind. I talk too damn much. I suppose it's because all I know and think has been cooped up so long. And then I was a couple up on you before you came. Ralph is all business. The only time I get to talk to him is on the phone. You wait, he'll be calling any minute now. As long as I'm home he thinks everything is all right." She leaned forward. The top of her pajamas sagged. But not her breasts. And no, she wasn't wearing anything underneath. She winked. "Is he right? About thinking everything's dandy just because I'm home?"

"That depends on how you look at it," I said cagily.

"Do you mind if I don't tell him you're here? Business can wait."

"Well, now, I don't . . ."

"Good. Because I'm glad you're here. There are things . . . I have my problems, too. And alone, I could slide into the wrong mood. I'll fix another drink." She took our glasses in one hand and pulled back the sliding glass door into the house. She turned back to me. "Are you sure she's only a friend?"

"Who?"

"That woman, what's-her-name?"

"Alicia? Mrs. McCabe?"

"You call her by her first name. Not very businesslike."

"You call me by *my* first name. Does that mean . . .?"

"Yes. But about the other. Strictly business?"

"Business."

"I'll believe almost anything. Tonight only. Because I want to. Tomorrow, I'll swear you're sleeping with her."

"Damn you. Shut up!" I said. But she was gone.

I had time to decide that I wouldn't trade a dozen like her for Alicia and a hundred for Bev. But I ordered my thoughts away from actively disliking her. It would show. And she might have her uses. I had caught her at the right time. There was an undercurrent of trouble behind her sharp talk. She was restless, dissatisfied and worried. It was ironic that I was always getting involved with women at the height of their tensions. But you go where the stakes are high and you always find trouble.

She came back with her Scotch and my bourbon and soda. It was mostly bourbon. She went inside and brought a telephone on a long cord, setting it on the terrazzo floor of the patio.

"Just you and I and the telephone," she said. "But don't let it come between us. Uh . . . Ralph, I mean."

"You don't like him. Why did you marry him?"

"None of your business. Oh, all right. Let's say it was convenient. There were certain advantages, even if I . . . even if they haven't materialized yet. Do you see anything attractive about his manly form, anything for me? Oh, he's not a bad guy, but . . . Let's skip it. You're destroying a mood. One I like."

"Just one question. Was he really a good friend to George?"

"McCabe? They were like partners. If George was alive . . ."

"What?"

"Nothing."

"Was he murdered?"

"I don't know. I'm not sure. In a way, I think he committed suicide."

"In what way?"

"I don't know. He drowned, didn't he? Nobody made him do that?"

"What about the detective or whatever he was?"

"I don't know. I don't know! Will you please, for God's sake, stop! Did you come here to pump me? Because if you did . . ."

"I came here to see Emory. Remember?"

She was silent a long time. Then the phone rang. She took it into the house and closed the door. I saw her lips move, but couldn't hear a thing. Her face looked strained and eager to please at the same time. She hung up. She disappeared inside the house. She came back with two bottles—bourbon and scotch. "Guess who that was?" she said.

"I can't imagine."

"He won't be back tonight. He's over at . . . but he'll phone a couple more times. You can count on that." She poured half a glass for me straight and the same for herself. For a long time she sat sipping her drink in silence. A sullenness had crept into her face. She showed no signs of being tight. But she wasn't the kind to show it. She was simply moody. All the time I kept planning little sneaky questions to ask her.

Suddenly she stood up, stretched and came over to my chair. She placed her hands on my shoulders, kneading with her fingers. She looked at me for a long time. "I don't know what to make of you," she murmured. "But does it matter?" Then she leaned down and kissed me. I tried not to let it get to me. Until then, I hadn't thought about her except objectively. Now there was a fleeting moment when I thought of Bev, and then Alicia. But Bev was gone to me forever. And did it matter now, this useless loyalty to the dead? 'Until death do us part.' And Alicia was still an unknown quantity in my life. But in all honesty, I'm not sure if I thought very much at all after the first moment or two.

Movie heroes are, at least in the end, loyal to their wives, girl friends, everyone around them. But in life, loyalty is largely dependent on circumstances. There is a lot of moralistic crap spoken, but the truth is that an honest-to-God man alone with a sexy, attractive woman who makes herself available, does most of his thinking later. It appears otherwise because circumstances favor loyalty. Most women need so much silly chit-chat and assurance of eternal love to rationalize over, a man seldom takes the risk or goes to the trouble. But Millicent Emory was not one who asked for tender platitudes, hand holding and a dozen dates filled with innuendos. She simply kissed me and didn't stop. Not long enough for thought. And the way she kissed didn't leave any room for thought. Or doubt.

My hands groped around her body in that automatic way that goes with her kind of kiss. She didn't object, but she didn't exactly respond. She moved away from me a little and said, "Did you know we have a pool?"

"No," I said, wondering what was coming. She took me by the hand to the other end of the back side of the house. She pressed a switch and soft lights glowed blue under the water of a pool shaped like Emory's desk. Kidney-shaped.

There were two little dressing rooms on the house side of the pool, a scattering of outdoor furniture, and a barbecue rig. "Want to swim?" she asked.

"Not particularly. I don't have a suit."

"Does it matter?"

"Well . . . Does it matter to you?"

"Ever swim in the altogether?" she said conspiratorily.

"Altogether what?" I knew perfectly well what she meant.

"Altogether nothing."

"Sure." I swallowed. I looked toward the house. It was dark except for a single light.

"The maid has gone," she answered my thought. "We can hear the phone."

I shrugged. "I'm game."

"Take the left dressing room," she said. "I don't need one." And with that, she undid her top and let it fall. Then she climbed out of the bottom part. She stood for an instant at the rim of the pool, pink and white where the sun never reached, the rest of her bronze. Smiling, she lifted her high, full breasts like a model posing, the nipples dark and as extended as they would be under an icy shower. Then she dove and knifed gracefully into the water.

I turned away with the utmost reluctance. I undressed quickly and dove in after her. She swam around me, splashing and giggling, her dark hair plastered against her face. She made a little plunge under water, then came up in front of me, paddling until our bodies touched. Her arms stole around me under water and she pressed against me. "God," she said. "This is going to be a night. A night I won't forget." I didn't have time to tell her she was right. I wouldn't forget it, either. Her body flowed over mine under water and she kissed me. There was the taste of the water and the taste of her mouth. Still clinging, we sank slowly beneath the surface.

CHAPTER ELEVEN

In one of the dressing rooms, Millicent, or Millie as I came to call her after the incident of the pool, produced bath towels. We dried each other, giggling and teasing in the strained way of children who have suddenly discovered their nakedness. Then Millie gave me a white terry cloth robe belonging to Emory and donned one like it. She went for the bottles and glasses and brought them into the dressing room. This time she closed the door and locked it.

The dressing room contained several pieces of wicker furniture, deeply cushioned. There were two big chairs with end tables and a kind of daybed with an arrangement of pillows, a standing lamp and a table lamp. She lighted the latter and pulled the curtains across the windows. There was an extension telephone with a switch arrangement. She cut the switch in for calls and poured another round—straight. Then she held up her drink in mock salute. We drank and she turned off the light. There was the muted sound of her body settling on the daybed. I curled up beside her.

She was a hungry and unbelievably skillful lover. But her skill was without tenderness. It left the body satisfied but the spirit empty. Time passed without the knowledge of time. We made sounds but we didn't speak. And then came the moment of separation when there is the greatest vacuum between lovers who do not love and the mind, free of emotion, is clear and sharp as moun-

tain air at dawn. Lying apart, you pull on your cigarettes
and grope for your drinks and you are thoughtful.

"Millie?"

"Uh-huh." Sleepily.

"What do you want more than anything else in the
world?"

"This. And money."

"Which comes first?"

"Right now? Money. This becomes available. Sooner
or later."

"And money?"

"It's never too available."

"I thought you had all you could ever need."

"Ralph has lots and looks for more. Ralph buys things
for me with it. But my own bank account wouldn't take
me one way to China."

"Do you complain?"

"Sure."

"And what does he say?"

"Wait till after the next big deal."

"And do you believe him?"

"I believe what I can see and touch."

"You can see and touch me."

"Huh!"

"We want to know what's in the box."

"Don't make me laugh."

"We'll pay to know."

"How much?"

"Fifty thousand cash."

"Fifty thousand!" She propped herself on one elbow.
"What's the catch?"

"Alicia gets her two hundred thousand and you get
one quarter—fifty thousand."

"And how does she get her two hundred thousand?
Out of Emory?"

"Yes."

"By knowing what's in the box?"

"Yes. We can't bargain if we don't know what we're bargaining with. He'll pay if he sees we know the value of what we're selling."

"Maybe. But it might be dangerous for you to know."

"How can just knowing . . . ?"

"Suppose the box contained incriminating documents. Or the crown jewels, or . . . or, say a crooked device of some kind? If you were Emory, would you want anyone to know?"

"No. But I'd pay and worry about that later."

"Later comes pretty fast. And I wouldn't want to be on the worrying end of Ralph Emory."

"That would be dangerous?"

"If he wasn't sure you wouldn't use the information against him."

"That's true. Every man for himself. Fifty thousand. Fifty thousand dollars!"

"To China and back with plenty to spare."

"But if he thought I told you . . ."

"He wouldn't. We'd tell him Alicia knew all along but was afraid to admit it."

Her snicker came out of the darkness. "Ralph wouldn't have any reason to believe, I know. He's never told me anything really. But you pick up a piece here and there and you end up with an inkling. For instance, if you knew the history of George McCabe, the line of work he used to be in, you could figure out part of it, maybe. And then you hang around here and you listen and you hear other things . . ."

"Tell me."

"For fifty thousand?"

"For fifty thousand."

She laughed. "Where's the money? Let me see it. I want to touch it."

"You'll touch it when Emory kicks in."

"Listen, Burty boy, I'm not dumb. I could probably get the rest of the pieces and put them together for you.

But I'll take my share now. Cash. And I'd want to be long gone from here when the fire works start. Whatta you think this is, kid stuff?"

I knew we couldn't get the money and wouldn't pay it if we had it. But I wanted to ride free aways by dangling the bait. "All right," I said. "But we'd want more than a guess for fifty thousand. We'd want a look in that box."

"You have the money?"

"No. But it's possible we could get it. Emory has the code that opens the box. Could you get your hands on it?"

"That would be risky."

"Fifty thousand is a lot of money. And all we need is a copy. Where do you think it is?"

"Probably he's got it in the . . . I could find it. You get the money."

"And you get the code. Then we'll talk business."

"All right. Until then, shut up about it. It makes me nervous. Let's have a drink."

"We had several drinks. At least, she did. I merely sipped mine and pretended to fill my glass again, pouring from a light in the connecting bathroom between the dressing rooms. After awhile she grew cozy again, in a drowsy way, and I pretended interest—until she fell asleep. Then I dressed quickly in the dark and stole into the house.

I went first to the den where I had talked with Emory. I drew the curtains and lighted the desk lamp. It was useless. All the drawers of the desk were locked. There was nothing else in the room that would hold anything. But, on a hunch, I began to remove books from the shelves. In a few minutes, I found it. A small safe set into the wall. Of course, it was locked and that was another dead end.

Next I made a quick survey of the bedrooms, checking bureau drawers and closets. I found nothing of interest.

But in one of the closets, I spied the slate-blue gabardine suit that Emory had been wearing when I talked to him. Obviously he changed before he went out. Without an idea of what I might find, I ran through the pockets. There was a jingling noise like loose change. He must have left in a great hurry because in the trouser pocket I found a set of small keys, the kind that might open trunks, cabinets—or desk drawers! I ran back into the den. Finally I found the right key and opened the desk.

It was a great disappointment. There were letters from brokerage houses, stacks of bills, a ledger with meaningless figures, insurance policies, writing materials and playing cards, among other things. The desk was in great disorder, as though someone had been looking for something in a hurry. The contents might as well have been dumped on the floor, then thrown back helter-skelter.

I looked through a dozen scraps of paper. There was nothing like a set of figures resembling a code. Under a pile of stuff, I found a colored photograph. It was a picture of the private detective who was shot, Millie, Emory and a slim, freckle-faced man with a mass of carrot-red hair. I didn't recognize him, though from bits of description Alicia had dropped casually, I was sure it was George McCabe. The picture was taken on a dock in front of about eighty shining feet of sleek yacht.

There was something odd about the scene or the people in it, something strangely out of place. What it was wouldn't come to me and I was studying the picture carefully, when in the distance I heard the repeated ring of a phone. That would be Emory getting through to Millie. She would be awake and wondering about me.

Quickly I put the photo back where I found it and locked the desk. Then I replaced the keys in Emory's pocket. On the way to the pool, I decided I should have kept the picture because it probably wouldn't be missed.

What was it that didn't seem right in that apparently innocent scene? Anyway, it was too late to go back.

Millie was cradling the receiver when I walked into the dressing room. "Where you been?" She sounded annoyed.

"You fell asleep," I said. "I walked down to the edge of the bay for some air. Just coming back to wake you."

"What's the matter with the air in here?" she said suspiciously.

I didn't give her the first answer that came to my mind. "This is the one place your boy Emory forgot to air condition," I said. "It's stuffy."

She smiled then. "He thought it was just going to be used for changing clothes. I'll speak to him about it."

"Don't bother."

"No trouble. He just called. He's not coming back until about noon tomorrow."

I looked at my watch. "Today," I said.

"Today, tomorrow. Why don't you spend the night?"

"Huh. People who check by phone can check in person. No thanks."

"What's the matter, Burty boy? Did we take the edge off your passion?"

"Enough so I can think again—and play safe."

She stood up and let the terry cloth robe she had put on fall open. "Maybe we can revive you." She came and put her arms around me. I noticed how tiny she was in bare feet. I was looking down at the blue-black top of her head, her hair still damp from the pool. She pressed against me and lifted her face. I kissed her and for a moment I was tempted. I held her away from me and closed her robe against the temptation.

"You'd better straighten up here and get in the house," I said. "I'm leaving. See what you can do about getting some information and the code. Think about it."

"You think about the money. Maybe I could find someone who could open the box without blowing it. I'll let you know when you get the money."

"Never mind finding someone to open it. There are enough dirty hands grabbing now. Just get the code."

"I'll try. Give me some time. Then call me. Call at night when Ja . . . when Ralph isn't here."

"What were you going to say, Jack? Whatever made me think I was the only one who came around after hours?" I didn't believe I was the only one and didn't care.

She gave me a quick, nervous smile. "You're the only one who counts."

"So long, Millie. I'll be in touch. And thanks for the . . ."

"For what?" she giggled.

"For the swim." I went out the door and didn't look back.

CHAPTER TWELVE

"You're awfully late," Alicia said. "It's after two in the morning."

"That one takes time. You have to drink her liquor and listen to her troubles. She can't be hurried."

"I hope you found her boring."

I didn't answer. I had a guilty feeling I couldn't shake and didn't understand. We were having coffee and toast in the kitchen of Alicia's apartment. I was very sober and dead tired. I was hardly able to keep awake on the trip back.

"What did you find out?"

"Nothing much. I offered her fifty thousand to get the code."

"Fifty thousand!"

"Don't be alarmed. I just wanted to see how much she knew and if that kind of money would open her up."

"Well?"

"I think she knows enough to guess a lot of it. And I think she could find out the rest. She might even get the code. She'll be trying. Actually, I was stalling. People think they're not telling you anything and they are."

"Did she hint at anything?"

"A couple of things. That George, your husband, might have committed suicide, drowned himself, that if we knew his past, we'd have the key to a good guess at what's in the box."

"What else?"

"She got a little tight and decided to go for a swim in the pool. While she was in the dressing room, I took a quick look around the house. I found the keys to Emory's desk."

"No! Anything there?"

"Nothing. Not a damn thing. Except a photograph."

"Of what?"

"George McCabe was tall and slim, wasn't he?"

"Yes. It was of him?"

"And he had red hair and freckles?"

"Yes."

"He was in the picture. So was the detective, Emory and Millie."

"Millie?"

"Millicent Emory."

"Oh. Excuse me!"

"Drop it, will you? She's not exactly the formal type. She told me to call her that. The postman probably calls her that, too, for all her front."

"Sorry. What about the picture?"

"Nothing. Just a group picture in front of a yacht.

But at the time something or someone seemed out of place. Before I had a chance to study it the phone rang and scared me out of there. It'll come to me. But listen, we've got to find out more about George McCabe."

"How?"

"Well. Let's kick it around. What did you do about the house in Washington? Sell it?"

"No. It's on the market with a realtor. It won't bring me much because it's heavily mortgaged."

"O.K. That's not the point. You still own it."

"Yes."

"You have a key?"

"I have one and the real estate agent has another."

"What about the workshop in the back?"

"It was heavily locked and I never could find a key. Besides, I left in a hurry."

"Doesn't it have a window?"

"No. Just a ventilator—a big fan."

"I think we ought to take a look inside. A locksmith can open it if necessary. Then we ought to make some calls around Washington and see what we can find out about where McCabe used to work."

"You mean actually go to Washington?"

"Yes. Fly. A quick trip."

"One of us or both of us?"

"Both. I might need some help. There might just be some scrap of information around you could locate, to say nothing of what's in the workshop."

"What about Emory meanwhile?"

"Let him stew. We won't be gone long and it will whet his appetite."

"When would we leave?"

"In the morning. This morning."

"You really think . . . ?"

"I really think."

"All right. I'm willing. We don't even have to tell any-one here we're leaving."

We drove to the airport in the convertible. I wasn't particularly worried about being spotted there. They wouldn't be watching for a box they knew was gone. They weren't. The flight was uneventful. And short.

We took a cab through the maze of neat, concentric streets to a modest residential district, arriving at a small, white frame house close to four in the afternoon.

The house had two bedrooms, a tiny living room, kitchen and alcove, a single bath and basement. The furniture was early American, well kept and tidy. I tried to picture Alicia there with George McCabe and couldn't quite make it.

We stood inside the door and Alicia looked around sadly. With a sigh, she slumped into a chair and dabbed at her eyes. "I'm sorry," she said. "It's . . . it's not that I'm sentimental exactly. But you do remember things and . . . and George, he . . . poor, poor mixed-up George." She lighted a cigarette. "Well, where do you want to look first?"

She stood up and studied the tip of her cigarette. She looked very forlorn. I put my arms around her. "I'm sorry," I said. "Once I stood around looking at what was left of my life in a house like this. So, I feel for you. But cheer up. It can't get much worse."

"I wonder," she said. "I wonder."

I kissed her and we held each other and suddenly there was an unspoken closeness that with a little time could develop into anything. But there never seemed to be time. "Come on," I said. "Let's look at that workshop."

I got it right away when I saw the heavy wooden door standing splintered and slightly ajar. "Looks like we're a little late," I told Alicia.

We were. The door had been forced. Except for a bench with a vise and an assortment of tools, the shack was clean. "How much other equipment was in here?" I wanted to know.

"Oh, lots! I can't say what, though. Boxes and . . .

and big bulky machinery I don't understand. Most of it was covered the time I was here anyway. But how could anyone take all that stuff?"

"Simple. You back a truck up late at night and start loading. You'd need two or three men, of course, a dolly and maybe a winch, depending on how heavy the stuff was. It must have been well thought out. How did he get the machinery installed here in the first place?"

"I don't know. But it must have been sneaked in while I was at work."

"Well, come on," I said. "We're wasting time here. By now that stuff will be—where? Miami, probably. In some warehouse, basement or garage. God! If I don't die some nastier way, I'm going to die of curiosity. Let's see what they did to the house."

If anything had been taken or ransacked in the house, they had been careful and neat. We couldn't find evidence that anyone had been there. We went through all of George's personal effects, his bureau, closet and desk, and finally the hall closet and kitchen cupboards. Nothing.

"What are we looking for?" Alicia said. "I mean specifically?"

"Any scrap of paper with his handwriting or figures. Where else can we look?"

"The basement. But I don't think . . ."

"Let's try it."

There was little in the basement but an old trunk, a few worn suitcases, gardening tools and some rubbish. We searched everywhere, finally strewing the rubbish over the floor, old newspapers, letters, ragged pocket novels, even torn, canceled checks. We looked through every scrap for nearly an hour. Finally I opened a pocket cook book and a scrap of an envelope fell out. I examined it. Part of a penciled phrase that looked like "Divide by 4," appeared. At first, I was about to throw it away. And then I had an idea. "Alicia!" I shouted. "This

may be it! Quick. Gather all the torn fragments of en-
velopes you can find. Lay them on this newspaper."

It took a long while but it was ten times as exciting
as a crossword puzzle. Finally we had all the pieces of
the envelope in proper order on the newspaper. We took
the whole thing upstairs, found some scotch tape and
put the puzzle together.

"Look here," I said. "The envelope has a Miami postmark and the return address is Emory's. McCabe must
have worked this out right after a letter from him. Then
he must have copied it, torn up the envelope intending to
burn the scraps with the rest of the trash."

"Thank God he was careless just once," Alicia said.
"Now what does it mean?"

"Get out your part of the code and I think I can tell
you."

I put the two together and figured. "So simple it's
ridiculous," I said. "When you have the complete code."
The divide-by-four scrap I found, when put with another scrap, turned out to be divide by 4-R and was the
first part of the code on the back side of the envelope.

"See, Alicia? It says divide by four. Which doesn't
mean a thing until you know *what* to divide by four.
Your first corresponding figure is 328. Divide by four
and you get 82. That will be the first number you dial.
The numbers you were given didn't mean anything to
me because they had three digits and the combination
dials only run from 0 to 99."

"What does the R stand for?" she asked excitedly.

"It could mean the position of the dial—right side.
But I don't think so. I think it means the direction of
turn—to the right. Your next number is 540. On the
envelope it says, 'Divide by 9-L.' And you get 60, turn
to the left. That's your second number. There are four
in the first group, four in the second. That's four turns
for each dial. Notice the second group are odd num-

bers. We don't have the number of turns so we'll have to assume one turn per number."

"I never have known much about combinations," she said. "But I get the general idea."

"Well, reduced to simple terms, it's this way. What you have are eight meaningless numbers, four numbers for each dial. You could play with them for a week and get nowhere. Emory has eight meaningless numbers with an equally meaningless instruction to divide. Divide into what? But put the numbers and instructions together and it's almost too simple."

"I get it," she said. "But which set of numbers goes with which dial?"

"I imagine you start left with the first group and then right."

"Do you think we've really got it?"

"Well, there's obviously some information missing. But we can figure it out with this. Come on! Let's get back there. Fast!"

We were gone in ten minutes and on our way to the airport. At one-thirty A.M. we were speeding to the canal where the box was hidden under fourteen feet of water.

CHAPTER THIRTEEN

WE PARKED THE CAR opposite the dock and cut the lights. We half ran across the empty lot. Darkness and the early morning quiet strengthened a feeling of urgency and tension. There was always the possibility the box might be gone. Or the place watched.

We didn't speak. The soft, crunching sound of our feet seemed amplified. I wanted to walk on tip-toe. Then there was the clack of our shoes on the dock. And when we paused, the hushed stir of water around the pilings. We waited, listening. We peered into the quarter-moon darkness. Nothing.

It was the last piling, right side, at the end of the dock. Quickly I stripped down to my shorts. I lay belly down on the boards and eased backward over the edge until my feet touched water. It was chilly, but not cold. Slowly I allowed my body to sink under the water. Using the piling as a guide, I found my way to the sightless bottom. My hand found the chain, fingers sought and found the big snap. I opened it and unwound the chain from the piling. Sucked by the bottom, the anchor held, then gave slowly toward me. Bursting for air, I reeled in. There! I felt the box at my feet. Then, with one end of the chain around my wrist, I floated upward. My head came out of the water and I spent a full minute gulping air.

I passed the chain end up to Alicia and she held it while I swam to shallow water and made my way back over the dock. Leaning over the edge, I took the chain from Alicia and pulled up. It was harder pulling straight up than over the bottom. But finally the box broke surface, then the anchor.

"Got it!" I whispered hoarsely.

I set the box and the anchor quietly on the dock. I freed the box from the chains. I dressed in a hurry. In the excitement, I didn't mind the dry clothes sticking to my wet body, the soggy shorts.

"We'll take the whole rig," I murmured. "Don't think we'll need it again. Leave it in the trunk." We carried the wet gear to the convertible and sped home. We took only the grey metal box, the locked, fabulous secret, to Alicia's apartment.

We sat in her living room, lights on, curtains drawn.

Alicia poured bourbon over the rocks with a trembling hand. We drank. And looked at each other. Then at the box, resting at my feet. I picked up the two scraps of paper with their codes and studied them. Silently, Alicia handed me the keys and I opened the top lid. There wasn't a drop of water underneath. I twirled the black, shiny dials experimentally.

"Walk to the far end of the room," I told Alicia. "Over there in the kitchen doorway." She looked at me questioningly but obeyed. "Just in case," I explained.

"In case what?"

"In case something goes wrong."

"Oh, Burt. Burt! Maybe we'd better not . . ."

"Just a silly precaution. There won't be any trouble."

She smiled feebly. I began to turn the dials according to the figures I had already worked out. When I had run through all the numbers, I looked again at Alicia. "Ready?" I said.

"I'm scared," she said. Her face was bleached. "I don't think I want to know."

"Come on, honey. Don't chicken now. This is it. This is it!" When she didn't reply, I lifted slowly on the lid. When it didn't give, I pressed up. Hard. It remained frozen. I sank back in my chair.

"That's not it," I said. "It won't open. Come on over and check these figures with me."

We went over and over it and found it right. "What about the sequence, the order of turns?" Alicia said.

"Should read from top to bottom, logically. But then he wouldn't have put the complete instructions on this envelope. Probably just the essentials."

"Try it in reverse," she said.

I did. I sent her across the room again and tried. Nothing. For over an hour we switched the sequence around, tried the dials individually and in unison, figured and refigured and came up with a still locked box.

"I'm pretty sure I know what must be wrong," I said finally. "Most combinations don't have just one turn for each number. Some have two or three turns."

"That must be the part he didn't write on the envelope," she said.

"We'll have to guess then. Suppose the even numbers called for two turns each and the odd one? Back to your kitchen doorway. It might work."

When she was set I cleared the dials and began again, two turns for even, one for odd. That didn't work either.

"Now I'm going to try two turns for even and three for odd," I told Alicia. I went through the cycle again. "O.K. Ready?"

She nodded. I lifted. The lid moved slightly under my fingers. Startled, I jerked in my chair. "Got it!" I shouted. And then I opened the box.

What I saw was about as valuable a commodity as the world has to offer. But for a moment, I was actually disappointed. It was money. Mere money. Crisp, new hundred dollar bills banded tightly together. From the size of the box, and the bills, it could be a fabulous amount.

"What . . . what is it?" Alicia said.

"Money. Just money. That's all." She came over. And then I lifted one of the stacks. It was only a very small, tight bundle. Something gleamed underneath. I pulled out all the bundles and dumped them on the sofa. The money was only a surface cover. What lay underneath gave me the real shock—when I understood it.

There was the glint of bright metal—chrome or nickel, in squares. There were two of them.

"What on earth . . . ?" Alicia said.

"I held the metal squares under the light. The answer was plain on their surfaces. "Don't you get it?" I asked.

She shook her head.

"Well," I said, "I've never seen anything like them. But I know what they are. These are plates."

"Plates?"

"You don't eat off them. You make money with them—stamp it out on paper. And if the impressions are good enough, you go out and buy things with the paper—until you get caught."

She looked at me in amazement. "Counterfeiting?"

"Right. And unless all the fuss has been about nothing very much, these will be damn good plates. Notice that they're hundred dollar denomination like the money in the box. They're covered with some kind of hard metal, chrome probably, to protect them from deteriorating in use. I read an article on it once. That's what makes them shine." I reached for one of the hundred dollar bills. "See how the front of this bill corresponds with this plate? Now I'll turn it over and we'll compare it with the second plate. See? Identical. This is the back plate. One plate stamps the front, the other the back."

"And these are counterfeit plates?"

"I don't imagine they're the originals."

"You think George made them?"

"Probably."

"And what about the money in the box?"

"Let's take a look at it." I held it under the light. "Looks perfect to me." I leafed through all the packages. The money had the same color and texture. There was some writing on one of the wrappers. I inspected it. "Look here. It says—'Fifty thousand sample turnout using enclosed plates.' There's your answer. Phony!"

She read from the wrapper, frowning. She stared at me. "George's handwriting," she said softly.

"I'm sorry," I said. "Now if we only had a genuine hundred dollar bill, I . . ."

"I've got one," Alicia said. "In my purse." She brought it to me. I pulled a note at random from a packet and compared. Her note was older but otherwise I couldn't detect a single difference. "Never saw anything like it," I told her. "These fakes are absolutely perfect to the naked eye—texture, color and workmanship. Amazing! Just hold it. I'll be back in a minute."

I went to my apartment. In my luggage I had a paper-weight that was also a magnifying glass. I brought it back. Again I examined the bills. "Even under a magnifying glass, I can't see any difference." She looked and agreed. We checked a dozen bills. One was as good as the other. The serial numbers were all different.

"Alicia," I said, "I've handled a lot of money in my business. And if these aren't the best counterfeits ever made, I'll eat them one by one. No wonder there are people who would do anything, including murder to get their hands on them. I think there is more to this than clever counterfeiting, too. Take this engraving of Franklin on the fake hundred. There aren't twenty-five artists in the world who could turn out that kind of work. And even so, one artist can't accurately imitate another. To say nothing of the fact that different people work on different parts of a plate, which makes it ten times harder to duplicate them. If these plates correspond with these bills, and I'm pretty sure they do, they're the most valuable counterfeits ever made. Bills like these might get all the way back to the Treasury before they were discovered. They would pass an ordinary bank and even a Federal Resesrve—unless I'm off base somewhere. And I've seen a good many counterfeits, including hundreds."

"But they *are* counterfeits?"

"Yes. I don't see how they can be anything else. Here are the plates."

"There goes my two hundred thousand," she sighed.

"Then you don't intend to sell them?"

"I like money, Burt. But I'm not a crook."

I stood up and put my arms around her. "You don't win the money," I said. "But if it helps, you're winning me."

"It helps," she said against my shoulder. "A whole lot. More than you know. But now what do we do?"

I poured another round and we sat down. "What do we do? That's a good question. First we examine our motives. There's no longer a financial gain. So we can chuck it and clear out in comparative safety. Or we can go on as before and with this as bait, see what happened to George McCabe and the detective, then turn it over to the police."

She shrugged. "If we weren't cowards when it came to making money—why should we run now?"

"Keep it up," I said. "You grow less wealthy but more likeable every day. Seriously, I think we should turn this over to the police now. But then everyone will clam up and the police will bungle. This whole deal will be a waste. And now if we get in a bad spot, these plates will buy us out. I hope . . .

"All right. I'm game. So whatta we do? We agree to Emory's terms and arrange a meeting. We bring the box. But the box contains—what? Not the plates or the money. We change the figures on the code a little. That gives us time to stall."

"What's the point?"

"I don't know. Not exactly. But Emory probably knows who his enemies are and who killed whom. The reason he's not talking to us or the police is obvious now. He has something to hide. The plates. If he talks, he gives himself away as, at least potentially, a counterfeiter. If he's pushed a bit, he may tip his hand. Or, we can use this fifty thousand in phony bills to bait Millie Emory. There are lots of possibilities. I can't think any more. Let's sleep on it."

I was about to put everything back in the box when I saw a label that had been glued to the bottom. I held the box up so I could read. Empty, it was still heavy. "Close and lock box to reset detonator." I showed it to Alicia. "Here's another one to think about overnight," I said. "For the time being, I'm going to put everything back in the box and leave it unlocked."

"Take the whole mess with you," Alicia said. "I don't want it around."

"Thanks," I said. "Your generosity overwhelms me. But I'll take it along. I have the perfect hiding place."

"Where?"

"In the john."

"I don't get it."

"You will. In the morning. And Alicia?"

"Yes?"

"I can't say I've exactly enjoyed myself. But I haven't thought about the . . . the accident, or Bev, in twenty-four hours. I mean, I don't think of Bev in the same morbid way. It's like being hit over the head with a hammer to cure heartburn. It's negative, but it works. And it isn't just this lousy game we're playing. The best medicine I've taken, I'm now beginning to realize, is you. Goodnight, Alicia."

" 'Night, Burt. And thanks."

I pulled the roll of bills—the thousand dollars she had given me—out of my pocket and dropped them on a table. "You're going to need this now," I said.

Before she could object, I left with the unlocked box containing its secret—former secret—under my arm. It was almost daylight.

CHAPTER FOURTEEN

In the morning, I borrowed some heavy friction tape from the manager. I lifted the lid of the toilet water chamber in my apartment and taped the plates securely to the bottom side. There were ten tight stacks of one hundred dollar bills, five thousand phony dollars to a stack. Carefully, I taped these over and around the plates, and replaced the lid. It was hardly conceivable that anyone but a plumber would lift that cover. Even so, the bills and the plates were concealed unless you turned the lid over. There weren't going to be any plumbers tinkering in my apartment without my knowledge. And I figured it was about as unlikely a place for anyone else to look as you could find.

Next I examined the box carefully for a clue to the mechanism that would detonate an explosion. Empty, the box was still heavy enough to contain most anything. There was a separation of about half a foot between the outer and inner containers. Room enough to conceal plenty of dynamite or some other explosive around the inner walls and still have space for some form of chemical or battery detonator. There wasn't a way in the world of telling what lay between the walls because heavy metal strips at the top connected the containers and prevented a view of the intervening space below. To tamper with the box, even open, might be just as dangerous. And highly unprofitable in view of the risk. There was nothing to be gained but the satisfaction of my curiosity. So I wrapped a hammer, a wrench and a tire iron in strips of cloth and relocked the box. I put the box in one of my suitcases, which I also locked, stowing it in the back of a closet. That would keep any amateur thieves from getting themselves blown all over my apartment.

I was about to go next door to Alicia when my phone rang. It was Millie. She sounded subdued. Almost frightened. There was none of the "Burty boy" manner in her tone.

"Burt?"

"Right."

"I sneaked out to call. I've got to see you."

"Why?"

"I have information. Do you have the money?"

"What information?"

"What's in the box."

"You're too late, Millie. I know."

"You couldn't. If you opened it the . . . You wouldn't be talking to me. You can't open it without the code."

"What did you hear would happen if the box were forced open, Millie?"

"I . . . Don't you know?"

"Sure. I want to see if you do."

"I don't suppose it makes any difference. I heard that there is some kind of explosive that would go off."

"Okay. I guess you know that much."

"And I know the rest—for dough."

"Alicia really did know, so you're wasting your time. She got the information in a letter McCabe left her in a safe deposit box."

"Don't kid me, Burt. What's in it then?"

"Gold boullion. Stolen gold." It was the same kind of trick I played with Emory in reverse.

"Nuts! It's nothing of the kind."

"Okay," I said. "Just wanted to see if you were stringing me along. It has something to do with money."

"Of course it has. What else?"

"Let's put it this way. If you had what's in the box, you'd also have to have some other equipment not near as hard to get, that goes with it. You could then set yourself up in business with a mechanical process that's crooked but would make all kinds of money for you."

"Huh! Sounds like you *do* know."

"I said I did."

"I'm still not positive. How many are there of these things and what shape and size?"

"There are two. They're square. About the size of— oh, say a dollar bill."

"Damn! They're plates, right?"

"Right. For counterfeiting. A very dirty little game, eh?"

"Everyone has some kind of racket. Burt, I don't like it, though. It smells of lots of trouble. I've got to have some money. Got to get away from here. I'm . . . I'm frightened."

"Of whom?"

"Never mind. Meet me somewhere and I'll tell you everything I know."

"Where?"

"Let's see. Do you know where the radio station is in Ft. Lauderdale?"

"Not exactly. I've seen the tower."

"It's on a side road about a mile or so toward the ocean from Route One. Look for the road pretty soon after you cross the draw bridge going toward Miami. Meet me in front. There's a boat yard nearby where we can park and change cars."

"Okay. How long?"

"About an hour."

"I'll be there."

"Do you think you can raise some money? Even a little?"

"We'll see. In an hour. So long." I hung up.

Alicia was asleep. She came drowsily to the door in a robe. "For heaven's sake, what time is it?" she said.

"After eleven."

"I could sleep another twelve hours. Come in and have some coffee."

She fumbled with the coffee pot, then went to apply make-up. She came back with a new face and wide awake eyes. "What's up?" she wanted to know.

"I have a date with our girl friend, Millie. She just called."

"Just called? How did she get your number?"

"I don't know. That's one thing I mean to ask her, among others."

"She must be anxious. What did she say?"

"She's not only anxious, she sounds a little desperate. She wants money. I think she wants to run someplace. She knows what's in the box and probably more. I did a little verbal fencing with her and when she was sure I understood about the plates, she opened up and admitted she did, too."

"God!" Alicia said. "Sometimes I think we were the last to know. So you're going to see her."

"Meet her. In front of the local radio station. She said something about changing cars and having a talk."

"You're sure that's all she ever does? Talk?"

"Alicia! I think you're jealous."

She smiled. "I think so, too. I've never seen her, but I don't like that woman."

"Neither do I. So don't worry."

She poured coffee and we sipped thoughtfully. "Burt, do you know we forgot something?"

"What?"

"We were going to make some calls about George when we were in Washington."

"I know. And I didn't forget. It was too late in the afternoon. If I can't squeeze Millie, I'll make some calls from here."

"Squeeze is an unfortunate word, Burt."

"Sorry. Pinch? Hug?"

"That's worse."

"We might even develop a sense of humor after this is over," I said.

"We might develop a lot of things."

"You mean?"

"I mean."

"Okay. That's enough. You're cracking my frozen face with all this levity. I might look in the mirror and not recognize myself. Cigarette?" She took one and we lighted up. "Alicia? Excuse the one track mind, but have you noticed something odd about this little situation?"

"Lots of things."

"I mean, well, suddenly some of the pressure seems to be off."

"How's that?"

"All right. A few days ago we were being chased all over the map because of the box. Guns were exploding, people were being killed, three goons were hunting me down—and then nothing."

"They don't know where we are."

"Maybe not. But they're a pretty industrious bunch to put it mildly. I think they might have had some line on us by now. Yet we come and go and I don't even have the feeling of being followed. All is peaceful."

"It is strange, come to think of it."

"Damn strange. We're suddenly unpopular. And when we find out why, we may have the key to something. If we ever do find out. When the war is still on and there's a sudden quiet at the front, I'm suspicious. When the enemy does nothing he's most sneaky. I think we're in for a storm, but I don't know where it's coming from." I looked at my watch. "Got to go." I went to the door. "Have that .45 handy and don't open this door unless you see my puss."

"I'll be careful."

"Extra careful. I sense trouble. So long, honey." I left.

I parked the Cadillac in front of the match-box radio station which sat on the edge of a canal, towered over by its transmitter. It was a back road, unpaved and overhung with trees. Isolated. Ahead a quarter mile, there was a dock with fishing supplies and gas pumps for refueling small boats and yachts. To the right of the dock there was a large boatworks where boats were made and sold. Next to this was a parking area containing less than a half dozen cars. I was wondering how Millie knew of this place when she drove up in Emory's Lincoln.

She beckoned me to follow her and when we pulled

up near the boatworks, she parked her car and climbed into the convertible. "Drive straight back the way we came," she said. "About a mile. Then turn right. I'll tell you when."

"How do you know about this place?"

"Believe it or not, I used to work for an advertising agency in Miami. I came down here with my boss once to stage a political program we were putting on various stations around Florida. Here! Turn right. It's desolate, but we won't be bothered."

We drove over a rutted dirt road for another half mile. The trees were so thick the road was almost obscured. We turned right again, at her instruction, dipping down to a small clearing by another canal. The water was stagnant and oily looking as though it never stirred. There was a battered old dock with rotting timbers. The grey hull of a half-sunken and water-logged cruiser nosed mournfully out of the water and listed toward us. There was nothing else—not a sign of a house or human being. The place was cool and damp and smelled of decay.

"Stop right here," she said.

"I'll have to. We're not amphibious, you know."

"How did you really find out about the box, Burt?"

I decided to be truthful. "We dug up the code and opened it."

"Where did you find it?"

"It's not important. To you."

"I searched the house top to bottom, but I couldn't find a thing."

"Then how do you know so much?"

"I told you once. I keep my ears clean. People come and they talk to Ralph and I listen. Long ago, I figured it wasn't safe not to know what's going on."

"Your rooms aren't very soundproof."

"You're wrong. You could stand outside the door of the den and not hear a word."

"So?"

"So from my room I can hear everything."

"Electric ears?"

She nodded. "Did you notice the radio in the wall of the den?"

"Yeah."

"There's another one like it in my room. They look innocent, but they play strange music. One listens and the other reports. It cost me three hundred and seventy-five bucks and a lot of sweat standing guard at the windows while the sets were gimmicked. But it was worth it."

"Can you trust the guy who did it?"

"So far. He doesn't know anything and he's dumb—except with gadgets. Besides, it was a long time ago, before . . ."

"Before what?"

"Before I got even smarter."

"Okay. So you can listen. What do you hear from the mob?"

"Don't be smart. I don't feel funny."

"Sorry. Now that I know this much about George McCabe, I want to know the rest. I have a curious mind."

"Will you help me?"

"There always has to be an angle."

"Yes. Even love has an angle. It wants something for what it gives."

"How should I take that?"

"Don't take it at all. Just an off-hand remark. I've never known much about love. That was good. Will you help?"

"Well, sure. If I can."

"I want to get out of here fast—jet propelled with a tail wind. I'd take the next rocket for the moon if I had money for a ticket."

"That bad?"

She nodded. I waited. There was the distant spatter of an outboard far up the canal. It died away and there was only the cloistered silence, the moist decay smell and the sad grey hull of the dead boat in the dead water. "If in this whole stinking world you could trust someone," she pleaded, "could I trust you, Burt?"

I looked at her suddenly and for the first time, I felt sorry for her. She was hard and bitter but she had probably never known an ounce of real love or affection. She had looked for love in love-making and hadn't found it. She compelled a little honesty from me.

"I don't know," I said. "I don't know if you could trust me or not. On some things, yes. It would depend on where we meet and where we fall apart."

"God!" she said. "My God, that's the first honest answer I've had from anyone in years. I think I'd rather trust you than all the glib liars around me. At least I know where I stand. Oh, Burt. Burt! What's happened to me?"

She fell against me and I looked down at her. Her lower lip trembled. For a moment the closed, careful look had left her face. Her eyes begged for the kiss and I gave it to her, without thought or desire, fulfilling her need. Her mouth against mine was, this once, tender and desperate for affection.

She undid her mouth from mine and whispered against my ear—"Burt, baby, we could have the world together. The whole world. We could get lost together and take it with us. I'd show you how."

I knew there was hidden meaning in what she was saying, but she was kissing me again in a different way and it became unimportant. She was so clever and so urgent with that marvelous body, she could make slaves out of men of her mentality. And she could make me lose my mentality—for a time.

She slid sideways against me. Her mood had changed. She had slipped back into the familiar pattern, the area she understood. I knew that now she was going to seek the only release she knew.

"Did you ever make love in a car, Burt?" she murmured.

"Almost everyone has."

"Did you like it?"

"I suppose. Yes."

"I like it best of all," she said. She pulled her tight skirt up over the cool, stockinged legs, exposing an inch or two of golden flesh. "You could see these legs on the beach, much more of them, Burt, and hardly notice." She teased the skirt up another inch or two. Her legs opened like oiled scissors and closed sharply. Watching, I felt like I had drunk a pint of port wine. "You put stockings on the same legs, cover them with a skirt, lift the skirt a little and you can't take your eyes off them. Can you, Burty boy?" Her knees toyed with each other, a silky, soundless sound. "That's what makes a car exciting, Burt. You see a bit here and a bit there and you want to see more."

I swallowed. "You can do that on a couch."

"Sure. But it doesn't seem as naughty. And cozy."

She took my hand and placed it on one bare leg. Slowly she slouched forward and my hand couldn't go anywhere but up over her thigh. I wanted to leap at her. I wanted to climb all over her. But my hand froze on the edge of abandonment. It's like any driving desire. Wait a minute and it'll diminish so you can bear it. I waited. I took my hand away and used it to smooth her skirt back down.

"What you were looking for a minute or two ago, you'll never find this way, Millie. It's only another trap."

"What a strange one you are," she said. "What was I looking for?"

"Skip it. Something you've never found and probably never will."

"It's that McCabe woman. Alicia. She got to you, made you go soft. Didn't she?"

"Maybe." I knew she was right. Otherwise you don't

turn down the Millies of the world. They're seldom around the next corner—just waiting.

"Listen, Burt. You don't want her. She's milktoast. Cold milktoast. You want excitement. And an ocean of money. I can give them both to you."

"What do you know about someone like Alicia? And where are you going to get this ocean of money when only an hour ago you were needing mine?"

"I've heard about Alicia. I think I know her type. Exciting like dishwater and laundry on a line. I know you, Burt. That's all I have to know. As for the money, bring me those plates and I'll show you where the rest of it is—the equipment. In a few days, we'll be able to compete with the Bureau of Printing and Engraving."

"You know where the equipment is? The printing press, the rest of it?"

"I know where there's equipment. All set up. Period. And the money we would turn out wouldn't be counterfeit. It would be real."

"Now you're just talking nonsense."

"Am I? I'll tell you something you don't know about George McCabe."

"I'm listening." I'd have heard a mosquito at fifty yards.

"Do you know where McCabe used to work?"

"I'm beginning to have an idea."

"He was a guard at the Bureau of Printing and Engraving in Washington. They make just one thing there. Money! All of Uncle's nice green currency."

"So?" I tried to sound casual.

"Do you know what else they make there?"

"No."

"Plates. The engraving plates that stamp out the money. They make a mould or a die or whatever you want to call it. And then from this die, by some complicated process I don't pretend to understand, they make copies and copies of these plates. They have to make a lot of copies because the plates wear out. Now let's suppose that a couple of these plates were stolen by a trusted employee—say hundred dollar plates. Can you imagine the possibilities?"

"No. Because I don't think it could happen. The plates would be so heavily guard—"

"Guarded! Ah. See what I mean? Who watches the chaperone? Who guards the guard?"

"I see what you're driving at. But you can bet your life the guards are watched, too. Are you trying to tell me George McCabe stole those plates?"

"I don't know. But we . . . I can't find any other answer. The plates are flawless. He never would tell how he got them. But how else?"

"Impossible."

"Impossible? Listen. I heard Ralph discussing it. Here's about the way he put it and it makes sense: For anything that man has conceived, any machine or gadget, there's a man who can figure a way to beat it, tear it down or copy it. Likewise, there isn't a security measure made by man to prevent a theft, that a man can't find a way around. Especially if he's clever and careful and patient. And that was George all over. Still don't believe it? Ralph gave a few examples. There's the Brink's robbery. Impossible? Sure, but they did it and got away with over a million. There's a guy in Indiana. He kills five people and they sentence him to the electric chair. They lock him up tight. Can he get away? Impossible. But he does. He makes a master key out of paperback novel covers and tin foil. He opens those doors and walks out free. Houdini did the impossible all his life. There's a gang who stole a safe with a lot of money. The safe was sitting right in a window. Cops walking by. How did they do it? Impossible? No. They cut out cardboard the same size and on this cardboard they did a painting of the safe. They put the cardboard in the window and stole the safe. Do you think it's impossible that money could be stolen from the Bureau of Printing and Engraving?"

"Yes."

"It happened. Right under their noses. Thousands of dollars. They recovered it because someone talked. But it happened. All these things happened. So what's impossible?"

"All right. It's possible. But there'd be a nationwide search. It would be in all the papers."

"You can't search for a dead man. At least you can't get much out of him. And don't think for a minute they'd release that kind of information to the papers. They'd work under cover with the Secret Service."

"Sounds logical."

"Another thing. Do you know what McCabe's father did?"

"No."

"He was an engraver. At the Bureau. And get this. The portrait of Franklin on the hundred dollar bill was engraved by him."

"Wow!" I thought I understood now why George McCabe had waited with his scheme until his father died. His strange brand of loyalty. "Is it possible," I said, "that McCabe's father taught him engraving?"

"It's not only possible, it's true. His father taught him all he knew. He had hopes that George would be an engraver, too."

"Then isn't it also possible that our boy George used his talents to make those plates himself?"

"Sure. There again, anything is possible. But the plates are so perfect it isn't likely. Takes more than one artist to make a plate and more than one machine. No one's ever found a way to make a perfect phony plate. But that doesn't mean it's impossible. We just don't know."

"He never said anything at all?"

"Not a word about that. He wouldn't open his mouth."

"Then the secret died with him. But he had a better

chance of making a perfect plate or stealing one than anyone I ever heard of."

"Yes. And you can't make a good bill without the right paper and ink. It's very special paper and the ink is made by master chemists. George had both the right ink and paper. Where did he get them if he didn't steal them?"

"I don't know. But this is the damndest, craziest business I ever heard of. I wonder . . . If the plates were stolen, that would be such a serious thing you'd almost think they'd call back the whole issue of hundred dollar bills, then make a change."

"Ralph spoke of that in one of his little meetings, too."

"You've known for quite awhile then."

"Yes."

"What did he say about the call back?"

"He said he didn't think they would unless the market was flooded with bills from those plates. It hasn't been yet and when it is, the plan is for releasing the bills over a very short period, a matter of days. And in various parts of this country and Europe through certain channels. Emory figures that's the way to beat it."

"He's thought of everything."

She smiled. "Just about. But you have the plates and we could take over the whole thing. You and I and a little reliable help I could get. It can't fail. It's the biggest thing of its kind in history. We'd be loaded for keeps. Everything in the world we want—ours. What do you say?"

"I say no."

"Why?"

"I have my own reasons. You might not understand them. But it's not for me—now or ever."

"Then for God's sake, help me, Burt. I can't go into it. But I'm in trouble. Real trouble. I've got to get out of here before . . . before . . ."

"Before what?"

"Can you lend me some money?"

"How much? I'm just a poor glorified clerk, you know."

"Five thousand, maybe?"

"Five thousand!"

"Well, I . . . I . . ." Her mouth hung open as though it were locked in place forever. Her eyes became hugely dilated with terror. I looked at her in amazement. I thought she was having a kind of stroke. Then I thought she heard something. I listened. Again there was the high whine of an outboard, distant and lonely. Then I thought she saw something. Her stare was fixed over my shoulder. I looked out the open window on my side.

They stood there very quietly. Their faces were blank—like soldiers on guard duty. They held their rifles like hunters—casually cradled in their arms. They stood shoulder to shoulder by the door, waiting. The big one with the yachting cap saw her spasmodic movement toward her door. He moved easily around the car and took up a position by her window. He carried no visible weapon. Like the others, his face was inscrutable and his eyes had the same look of bored efficiency.

I had never clearly seen the two with the rifles. But they were of the same build and they were with the stocky one. I knew it was the trio of the Miami airport chase. I also knew that I wasn't going to get to run this time, that I wouldn't even try, that death was outside my window and it had come to stay. Mentality left me. Fear filled the vacuum. I could feel Millie's leg trembling against mine.

The one with the cap opened Millie's door. The gun in his belt looked like a .38. With a small, backward tilt of his head, he motioned her out. She looked at him and then back at me. "For the love of God, help me, Burt," she whispered hoarsely—as though even to break the silence would spell her doom. Her terrified face was one great pathetic plea.

"You'd better go, Millie." Even then I wasn't sure it

was I who had spoken. The voice seemed to come from outside me. She gave me a final look, almost of one betrayed, as if she thought, *Even you, even you.* And then she climbed slowly from the car. The door shut behind her, and the big one took her away by the arm—not roughly, not gently. He simply took her.

I looked at the other two. They stared back unblinkingly. When they moved away from the car, my mind whirled for a fragment of plan and found none. I waited for the rifles to come up, the whip snaps of the shots. But to my amazement, the big one came up with the girl, the two with the rifles took places on either side and the four moved off, up the road, their backs to me disdainfully.

The big one walked in advance. Millie, between the rifles, followed. The rifles were held at port and the men moved easily, but with a certain precision and without speech. Millie slouched along pitifully between the guards, her head held at half-mast. The whole thing reminded me vaguely of a detail of soldiers taking a prisoner to an execution.

Above the clearing on the road was the dark Buick. One of the riflemen held the rear door open. Millie entered and the man followed. The other with the rifle climbed in from the far side so that Millie was again between them. Then the big one took the wheel. They drove off without haste. Not an eye looked back.

I sat there for a long time, staring numbly at the grey, mossy hull. The outboard sputtered once and died. I wanted to hear it again. Any man-made sound. But the silence was profound. Then I started the motor and swung back onto the road, driving in a dream and with no more haste than the Buick.

<h1 style="text-align:center">CHAPTER FIFTEEN</h1>

"THE THING I don't understand," Alicia said, "is why they took what's-her-name, Millie, and left you alone."

"That's the all-time mystery," I said. "I swear, I wouldn't have given a Mexican jumping bean for my life."

"Poor Millie," she said.

"Yes. Poor Millie. I think she was playing too many angles and too many people at once."

It was the following morning, Florida at its best—immaculate sky, bathtub temperature, tropic wine fragrance in the air. We were driving along Route 1 on our way to Emory's. "The Box," as we had long since come to call it, was in its original black case which lay innocently on the back seat of the convertible. Alicia had phoned Emory and said she was at least willing to discuss price. Emory had said that he wanted to inspect the box before closing any deal and that we were to bring it along. On my instruction Alicia had agreed hesitantly, a thing we would never have allowed if we had not made the contents as bogus as the currency and plates it had originally held. We had also changed a few figures of the code around so that it could not be opened. And we planned to stall even an attempt to open it as long as we could.

As expected, Emory had been most cordial, hardly concealing his excitement. Alicia had purposely asked if his wife would be there, saying she had heard much

131

about Mrs. Emory and was anxious to meet her. There had been a long silence, after which he said, "Since you're going along with me on this thing, I'll be perfectly honest with you. Millicent has . . . has disappeared. I'm terribly worried. I've notified the police, but as yet they haven't been able to find a trace of her. I think it has something to do with the thugs who have been trying to steal the . . . the box. Of course I didn't tell *them* that—the police. But if she doesn't return . . . well, I may have to. We aren't exactly close, in fact frankly, we've been on the brink of divorce. But this is entirely another matter. They'll be trying to get the hiding place of the box out of her and the poor kid hasn't known any more than I have up to now. She doesn't even know what's in it."

Well, somehow his honesty made us feel better. We weren't so reluctant to deal with him as we might have been. I toyed with the idea of telling him what really happened to Millie, leaving out certain details of course, but decided to wait and see how he would react when he found out the box couldn't be opened.

And now we were just a couple of miles from Emory's and Alicia was saying, "I suppose there wasn't a thing in the world you could do to save Millie."

"Nothing. Nothing I could think of. I've been sick over it. But I was unarmed, there were three of them and I was pinned in the car. Surrounded. I'm not particularly brave. And there comes a time when it's foolish to try to be—when it would get you nothing but a bullet in the head. And they knew it. They walked away so disdainfully, with their backs to me. For a minute I had the wild idea of trying to run them down. But it was so quiet, they'd have heard me start the car—and then, of course, Millie would have been in the way. It was hopeless."

"Why didn't you chase after them?"

"And do what? Force them off the road? Besides,

they're not dumb. They'd have been watching for just that and I'd have been picked off before I got even close. It was useless. But still, I can't help feeling guilty."

"Don't feel guilty, Burt. You showed good sense. And she got herself into this. I'm glad you didn't take the pistol. You'd have gotten into a gun fight and then . . . I hate to think of it."

"I've got it with me now, though. I don't see any·reason to trust Emory much more than anyone else mixed up in this deal."

"Why? George said in his letter that Emory wasn't above making a fast buck. But he also said that he had known Emory a long time and that in his own way he was absolutely honest."

"You believe that?"

"Yes. Absolutely. George was a funny guy with strange ideas—dangerous ones. But his judgment of people was flawless. He never made snap decisions about them. And when I did, he would say, 'Don't ever say anyone is thus and so until you've known them at least two years and under circumstances when their weakest, most vulnerable sides are exposed.' I think he knew all there was to know about Emory before he trusted him with anything like this."

"Well, of course, I didn't know George. But from what you say, I'm inclined to agree. The only thing I have against Emory is that he would be willing to turn a crooked buck with those plates. Still, I don't suppose anything short of millions would have tempted him. I've always said, if I were going to steal, I'd steal a million or more and be done with it."

"Yes. And we don't know what pressures he's under. He may be in some kind of financial jam. Not that I excuse him."

"He did say he'd had reverses. And I suspect they were serious ones."

"Maybe that's the real reason he could only offer fifty

thousand. Maybe he couldn't raise any more and didn't want to admit it."

"It's possible. Though he did write a check for two hundred thousand."

She lighted a cigarette from the dashboard lighter, blew smoke out the window. She frowned. "I forgot about that. He's a mystery. But George loved me too much to take chances. Emory meant to go through with it and I think he can be trusted."

"Within limits."

"Of course. And I don't even know him. You do."

"You will in a minute. Here's our turn."

Ralph Emory came to the door himself. He wore white flannel trousers, one of those Hawaiian, flowered sport shirts, and a dark blue jacket. His smile was friendly, but I could see right away he was under a strain.

"So you're Alicia," he said. "After all this time. You know, when we weren't discussing business, George didn't talk of much else. How are you, Keating? Both of you, come right in."

We followed the mass of his back into the familiar den. For the first time, I carried the black case without dread. I set it down by my chair and Alicia took a seat next to mine. Emory sat on a corner of the kidney-shaped desk and towered over us. "It's a little early for a drink," he said. "But if you . . ."

"No thanks," Alicia said.

I shook my head in the negative.

Emory was looking at the case. "Then do you mind?" he said. "I'd like to have a look."

I passed him the case. "It's open," I said. "The case, not the box. Go right ahead. Unless you have any objection, Alicia."

"None," she said.

The case snapped open. He looked inside a moment, then carefully lifted the box. I watched him closely. His face was bland. But a muscle in his jaw worked and betrayed his excitement.

He studied the box, turning it over slowly. "You know," he said, "George showed this to me once before This is it all right." He laid it on the desk. "I'd offer you a cup of coffee, but my girl is off today." Then to Alicia, "You have the code that goes with the one George gave me?"

Alicia nodded and began to open her purse. I held up my hand. "Don't you think we ought to discuss the terms first?" I said.

He smiled. "You see, Alicia?" he said. "You're too trusting. You should be very grateful to have a man like Keating on your side." He sat down behind his desk and assumed a ready-for-business air.

"Of course I am too trusting, Mr. Emory," Alicia said. "But on the other hand, George said in a letter he left me that you were the only one I could trust. He seemed to trust you more than me because he wouldn't even tell me what was in the box."

Emory considered the nails of one manicured hand, looked up. "It wasn't that he didn't trust you, Mrs.— Alicia. Mind if I call you that? It seems I've been doing it."

"I don't mind," she said.

"It wasn't that he didn't trust you. It was more that he felt you might not want to sell the box at all if you knew what was inside it."

"I don't understand."

"The box contains something that has to do with . . . well, let's say, for the sake of argument, something to do with gambling. Because," he smiled ironically, "it will be a very large gamble. Gambling is, in some cases, just the other side of the law. Do you approve of gambling, Alicia?"

"I neither approve nor disapprove, so long as I'm not involved with it."

"There! You see? As long as you're not involved. In the same way, George didn't want you to become involved with something that might be construed as—well, to put it nicely, and very loosely, borderline."

"I think I see what you mean," Alicia said. "Mr. Emory, if you were a friend of my husband's, aren't you interested in finding out what happened to him? For the sake of my own conscience, I'd like to know myself."

"I'd not only like to know, I think that I *do* know. At least I have a pretty good idea."

"Tell me. Please!" she said.

"I can't tell you anything until I have positive proof. No use running to the police with guesswork. They've exhausted every possibility. But I have other avenues. And as long as you don't see gambling in too bad a light, I might be able to tell you, not what I know, but what I'm trying to prove."

"Anything at all, Mr. Emory."

Emory lighted a cigarette and stared reflectively at the curl of smoke. "It's a funny thing about gambling," he mused. "Here in Florida we have race tracks going full tilt much of the time with millions being won and mostly lost, I'll admit. But though it's perfectly legal to bet on the horses, you can't bet off the track and you can't play cards, shoot dice or operate a roulette wheel. Yet the same principle is involved. Does that make sense?"

"It doesn't seem to," Alicia said. "What are you driving at?"

"I'm answering your question in a round-about way. First I have to justify myself. I don't suppose it was any secret between you that George was a great gambler."

"He told me."

"He preferred other forms of gambling to horses. And I think he'd have spent more time in Vegas than Florida, if Florida wasn't closer to Washington. See what I mean?"

Alicia fidgeted in her chair. "Not quite."

"I told your friend Keating I was a speculator. That's a rather euphemistic word. Actually, you see, I'm a gambler. On the right side of the tables. I own, or did own, several, shall we say back-room gambling casinos. That's where George did his gambling. But very recently, there was a change of local politics. And the new regime took a dim view of my enterprises. In short, they recently closed me down. Perhaps that explains why I'm a little low on funds. In fact, I'm scraping the barrel." He looked around the room. "And, as you may have noticed, my overhead is high. I even had to let go all but one servant. There is this house to maintain, two cars and a large yacht. And if Millicent, God help her, remains with me, she has expensive tastes. Now, perhaps you see one of the reasons, the principal one, why I have to quibble about money for the box. I just don't have it. On the other hand, for the very reason that I don't have it, I need this box desperately. Otherwise," he sighed, "I'm not sure I'd want to touch it at all. It's proved to be very bad business, so far. It's cost two men their lives, my wife has been kidnapped, and it may cost me a lot of trouble—and a lot of time." His smile was sardonic. "And I don't mean time under the Florida sun."

Alicia said, "I still don't see what that has to do with George's death. Although, I understand why you can't pay what you had promised."

"I'm coming to that. A gambling enterprise such as the one I was in, took a lot of capital. And help. The man I chose as a partner had the capital, and a certain know-how. But he also had, and has, some rather dubious qualities. I draw the line in certain places. He draws the line at nothing. It was a little too late when I found that out. We no longer do business together. But his name is Jack Cannova, he's a former syndicate boss and pretty much an underworld character. And unless I'm a total idiot, he's behind the death of your husband, the investigator and my wife's kidnapping. I don't have his connections, but I've got some pretty good boys who used to work for me at the casinos, checking him. And when I get some concrete evidence, I'm either going to handle him myself or turn it over to the police. Of course, I'm pretty much a lone hand because I'll admit I don't stand very high with the local gendarmes. And that's the story, in as much detail as I can give you right now. Except that I mistakenly told Cannova about the box. I needed his help. That was more than a mistake. That was suicide."

"He knows what's in the box?" I asked.

"Yes. And he'd do anything to get it."

"Well," I said. "Alicia described the men who shot the investigator. They're three big boys, the leader especially. He always seems to be wearing some kind of yachting cap. I had a run-in with them myself."

Emory nodded sagely. "That would be Dan Halloran and his helpers. They run a charter boat out of Miami —fishing. But they also do some smuggling from Cuba and they work for Cannova. They're his strong-arm crew, among other things."

That was a real shocker to me. Right then and there I was tempted to tell him what happened to Millie by the canal. But the phone rang.

"Excuse me," Emory said. "Hello. Yes? This is Ralph Emory. . . . What! You have? . . . Thank God! Where did you find her? . . . I see. Well, good work! I'll wait right here." He hung up. "That was the police," he said. "They found Millicent. They wouldn't say where. She's been beaten up, but she's not seriously hurt. A squad car is bringing her right over. God! Oh, God. What a relief."

"I'm so glad!" Alicia said.

"To tell you the truth, I didn't expect you'd be seeing her again, Mr. Emory. You're mighty lucky," I said.

"Just as long as she's alive," he moaned. "We can straighten out anything."

After that, conversation died. Emory kept drumming his fingers on the desk, answering tersely. I gave Alicia a look and we shut up. He wasn't going to talk until after Millie arrived. I think I was almost as relieved as he was. Much of the guilt over our affair and her kidnapping left me.

In a matter of five minutes, the doorbell rang. "That will be the police," Emory said. He left on the double.

I heard the door open and there was the murmur of voices, Emory's strident over the others. Then there was the clump of feet coming toward the den. Emory entered first. He looked flushed and at the same time, frightened. I say he entered the room. Actually, he was shoved in. The three men who followed did not wear uniforms and they were not police. It was the third time I had seen them and the sight was sickening. Because the man just behind Emory held a .38 in his back and wore a yachting cap. The other two, of course, were the rifle detail who took Millie. They carried snub-nosed .32's. The one Emory had called Halloran pushed him into a chair, where he sat so watchfully, his jaw working so steadily over some controlled emotion, I almost expected him to spring up and start throwing his big bulk around. But I knew by his eyes that he was more scared than he was angry.

One of Halloran's boys got to me just as I was cautiously slipping my hand into my coat pocket. He took my .45 and shoved it into his hip pocket without a word. Then the big one, Halloran, tucked the box under his arm. He swung the .38 on me. "I'll take the combination," he said. I was so used to thinking of it as a code, I looked at him blankly a moment. "Come on, hurry it up," he said and followed with a sharp boot in the shins that half lifted me out of the chair and made purple lights explode before my eyes.

"I've got it," Alicia said. She opened her purse and produced the doctored card with the code. He snatched it out of her hand and tucked it in his shirt pocket. He started to leave the room, followed by the others.

"Halloran!" Emory called. The big one hesitated, turned. "You dirty sonofabitch," Emory said evenly. "You big, gun-happy slob. Tell Canonva to have my wife back here in an hour, or I'll come down with my boys and take him apart."

Halloran took one long stride back into the room. The butt-end of the .38 came down savagely on the bridge of Emory's nose. It was a glancing blow or it would have crushed his nose like matchwood. Halloran turned with his usual disdain and left the room, followed by the others.

Emory mopped at his nose with a handkerchief. "The dirty bastard," he mumbled. He seemed dazed, but after a moment, he got up and staggered over to his desk. From a drawer he produced a shiny .45, similar to the one taken from me. I wondered why I hadn't seen it the night of Millie and the pool. Probably he had it with him.

Emory seemed now to be under control. For all his size, he ran nimbly from the room. I heard the front door open and, in a moment, close. For a couple of minutes, there was silence. When Emory came back to us, there was a band-aid on the bridge of his nose. "Gone," he said. "Gone. Naturally! And I know where."

"Where?" Alicia said breathlessly.

"Cuba. That's where Cannova is. And that's why I haven't been able to get him. They'll be taking the box over there. And Millie will be with them. Unless . . . unless she's dead."

"How will they go?" I said. "Fly?"

"No," Emory said. "They'll take the boat, the charter boat. And if I know them, Millie will be locked on board. If I don't stop them, they'll get rid of her at sea.

I'm sorry, but I'll have to leave you. And I don't know when I'll be back."

"What are you going to do?" Alicia said.

"I'm going to follow them. On my yacht."

"Can you get some help?" I asked.

"Haven't time."

"Don't you have someone on board?"

"No. Not anymore. And God knows where I could find anyone. My bunch have drifted away since the tables closed. A couple that were loyal I sent to Cuba to check on Cannova."

I looked at Alicia and spoke to Emory. "I'd better go along with you," I said.

"My God!" Emory said. "You're all right! Would you?"

"You're not going to leave me here alone, are you?" Alicia said.

I glanced at Emory. "I'd hate to do that," I said.

"Bring her along then. She can stay below, out of the way." He gave Alicia a kindly smile. "It wouldn't be any picnic, though."

Alicia bit her lip. "I'm going," she said. "I couldn't stand it here. And I might be of some help."

"I don't like bringing her along," Emory said. "But I haven't time to sit around discussing it. Both of you come, or stay. As you like."

"We'll go," Alicia said. "No more talk."

On the way out the door, I asked Emory, "How fast is your boat?"

"A lot faster than theirs. Even if they were at sea this minute, I'd catch them. Come on!"

We hopped into the Cadillac and tore away, swinging left on Biscayne Boulevard toward the harbor. I didn't like it. I didn't like it at all. I had the feeling we shouldn't bring Alicia. I had the feeling that we, even Emory with his knowledge, were running after something that was going to swallow us up as inevitably as it had been going to from the very beginning.

CHAPTER SIXTEEN

DURING THE DASH for the dock, I berated myself for having relaxed my guard. Because I knew the box now contained nothing of value, it had not occurred to me that Alicia and I were the only ones aware of it. We had been relaxed. We had not been watching and we had been followed.

"I suppose the phone call about your wife was a phony," I said to Emory.

"Probably Halloran," he mumbled. "Just a gag to get me to the door off balance."

"We may be able to catch them," I said. "But they're not exactly going to heave to and run up a white flag. They seem plenty capable."

"I've got something on board that will take the argument out of them," Emory said.

"What's that?"

He didn't answer me. He didn't speak again until he said, "This is it. Turn left here, then go straight to the bay."

The dock where Emory kept his yacht was just off Biscayne Boulevard, only a short distance from the pier of the charter fishing boats. I wondered why Emory didn't check to see if Halloran's boat was gone. But he seemed certain of what he was doing and in such a terrible hurry, I didn't bother him with questions.

Emory's yacht was called the *Barracuda*, a long, white sliver of burnished mahogany and brass—about eighty feet of speed and luxury. It boasted a flying bridge and two sleek launches suspended from davits port and starboard amidships. It was a little narrow for rough weather, sacrificing beam for speed. The large afterdeck was canopied all the way to the fantail, and dotted with deck chairs, including the sturdy swivel type used for sport fishing.

Emory piled out of the Cadillac first. He was already on board at the controls in the wheel house as we approached. I helped Alicia down the short ladder to the deck. She was hardly on board when I heard the big twin screw motors catch and hold. Emory stepped out on deck and shouted for me to cast off. I unhitched the ropes from their cleats fore and aft and leaped on deck. The yacht was headed seaward. The dock slid past slowly, then faster as we gathered speed.

Alicia was sitting in one of the deck chairs aft. I joined her. She looked grim and I felt edgy, so we didn't speak. Toward the end of the dock there was about thirty feet of Chris Craft cruiser. Two men and a woman stood beside it. A little girl was taking their picture. The man to the left of the woman had his arm around her waist in a tight, affectionate embrace. The other man stood a little to one side, awkwardly, as though he felt he didn't belong in the picture at all. The little girl held up her hand for them to remain motionless and then became intent with her small, square view of the scene. She joined them, winding the camera.

It was an unimportant little tableau and in a minute they were mere specks boarding the cruiser. But even after they were out of sight, a close-up view of the man who stood awkwardly to one side of the couple who looked like man and wife, remained with me like an image engraved on the retina. It was as though I held a picture of them next to the one I had taken from Emory's desk—and compared. There was a certain remote similarity. The man who seemed out of place on the dock, suddenly became Emory in the photograph. And then, instantly, I knew. And it was the most shocking knowledge of the whole affair. The man with his arm around Millie had not been Emory, but the investigator who had posed as Emory. Emory was the one who stood a little to one side with George McCabe. When the meaning became clear to me, I had a crawling sensation like one who is trapped in a speeding automobile about to crash headlong.

I could feel the throb of the engines close to full speed. We were piling foot hills of foaming water astern. An outboard rocked dangerously in our wake. The Miami shoreline diminished and began to be seen through the wrong end of the telescope.

"Alicia," I said, pushing my voice against the bubbling exhaust but not looking at her. "We're in trouble. Plenty of trouble. I haven't time to explain. But our big friend is not Emory. I'd gamble a swim back that he's Cannova."

She looked at me open-mouthed, her eyes wide and unbelieving.

"Don't ask questions, just believe me," I begged. "Can you swim?"

"A little," she said. "Not well."

"Then we'd never make it, even if we could get away with it. Sit tight, watch me and be ready for anything."

"Are you sure . . . ?"

"I will be in a minute."

I got out of my chair and started pitching toward the wheel house. Emory turned and saw me. A slow smile spread over his face. He pointed toward the flying bridge. I looked up. Halloran, the barrel-chested one with the yachting cap, looked down. In the crook of his arm, he cradled a Thompson submachine gun. It was a weapon I was very familiar with. On Saipan I had seen one like it cut the leader of a Jap patrol in half with one long burst. Call it a tommy gun if you like. Whatever you call it, stay on the butt end of it.

The other two came slowly from below, carrying the inevitable rifles. They took easy positions on the deckways at either side of the wheel house. They were unnecessary. When I saw Halloran with the machine gun, I knew it was all over.

CHAPTER SEVENTEEN

I TURNED AROUND and went back. I sat down next to Alicia. "You saw?"

"Yes," she said. "And I'm so scared I . . . Those are the men who killed the investigator."

"No. Those are the men who killed Emory. There never was an investigator. We're in for a rough time." She reached for my hand. I squeezed it. "Don't worry," I said. "We'll find a way out of this one, too." I knew we wouldn't. I knew we'd be dead before the day was gone.

"If they have the box and they think the plates are in it, what do they want with us?" she said.

"Probably just trying to throw a scare into us. And don't forget, we do have the plates and we can bargain with them. Nothing will happen to us while those plates are hidden in my john."

"Could they find them?"

"I doubt it. They're fastened under the lid of the toilet."

"I'm still scared. I can hardly breathe," she said.

"Don't use yourself up. Keep sharp. Watch for some kind of break."

It was just talk. I was sick with fear myself.

On our port side, the causeway to Miami Beach slid past. A stream of cars came and went to their vacation pleasure. Occasionally someone waved. The sun was high and bright in the sky and the day was built for sailing. I knew the wavers envied us our luxury, a beautiful yacht, a beautiful girl, the thrill of big game fishing. How casual, how relaxed, how grand we must have seemed to the beach-goers from the safety of their cars, lounging there together on the fantail, our crew, guns hidden now, standing easy but watchful of our every wish, our captain at the helm.

Shortly we left the palm-dotted causeway behind. Miami Beach came and went and we were out to sea, the ocean unfittingly placid, as though it was all a bad joke and now it was time to break out the beer and sandwiches. In the distance, we saw an occasional fishing boat trolling, outriggers extended, toy fishermen oblivious with their incongruous little sport. And when there was nothing but the bubbling blue-green glass and the glare of sun on its empty surface, the hulking one we called Emory came aft from the wheel house wearing his nose patch, sunglasses and a self-satisfied, almost friendly expression. He pulled up a chair facing us and sank into it, removing the glasses and rubbing the bridge of his nose tenderly, while studying us like two quite harmless, but interesting specimens recently dredged from the sea.

"All right," he said fatuously. "Let's get reacquainted. I'm Jack Cannova. Leaving out a few small details, the rundown I gave you on my background is quite accurate. If that doesn't convince you the shell game is over"—he looked up to the bridge where Halloran sat smoking watchfully, the submachine gun resting across his lap—"just remember on what side of that gun you sit." He paused to shove a cigarette between his beefy lips and light it, time enough for me to look around and see that one of the rifle boys had come to sit just a few feet behind us, weapon across his knees, the other having taken the wheel.

Cannova puffed smoke from his mouth and pulled a piece of tobacco from his lip. "Let's understand each other from the start," he went on. "Your chances of escape are just about nil." He made a wide gesture, obviously enjoying himself. "Around you nothing but ocean, upsettingly deep and filled with all sorts of rather unfriendly creatures, sometimes curious, mostly just hungry.

"Now let's take for granted that you can swim, and that anyway you'd like to try. Don't. It's about twelve miles to shore and at thirty-two knots, the distance is growing more ridiculous every minute. Soon you'll need a compass or some knowledge of celestial navigation to find it at all. The water is full of minor irritations like slimy jellyfish the size of a poker table, Spanish men-o'-war that suck to the flesh so tight they sometimes have to be cut away, and major ones like manta rays the size of grand pianos, sharks any size the mind can imagine and barracuda with teeth as long and sharp as hypodermic needles and twice as busy, to name a few. There's a fair chance you might not be bothered at all. Stories of man-eating fishes are exaggerated. But there are skeletons at the bottom of the ocean that never got to figure in the statistics." He paused, looking out to sea, dragging on his cigarette, having a wonderful time.

"But compared to our friends with the rifles and the tommy gun, this is a tale for children. They'll let you get your feet wet because this is a nice clean ship and we can't have a messy deck. But once in the water, they'll chop you in fish-size pieces before you get fifty feet. And their eyes never grow sleepy or careless because they are Navy trained and they understand my special brand of discipline. Now, on the other hand," he smiled broadly, "if you behave yourselves, you might get a chance to overpower us, as they do in grade-B movies, take our weapons and turn us in for the handsome reward. You'll have to be quite patient though, and watch for just the right opportunity. Don't rush it . . . And now the briefing is over. Keating, I'll take the original copy of the code to the box. And don't give me any goddam crap about it."

"I haven't got it," I said. "We left it behind."

"The hell you haven't! You want us to turn you upside down until we find it?"

"Look, Cannova. I'm not stupid. I know what you can do. I haven't got it."

"I'm going to believe that for the time being. I'll get you paper and pencil and we'll see how fast you can remember."

"I don't remember at all. It's very complicated. We doctored every one of the figures." I might have been able to remember most of it but I needed to stall.

"We could torture you, Keating. And you'd find that all that stuff you read about hard guys who take it for hours on end and never open their slobbering mouths is a lotta pure crap."

I knew he was right. Anyone can draw paper heroes. The real ones are mostly dead. "I'd probably tell you anything I know, Cannova. You're right. But I don't remember more than a couple of figures on that code."

He looked at Alicia. "Is your memory any better, cutie?"

She shook her head. I don't think she was able to speak.

Cannova leaned back and considered. I had a hunch he was one who would come up with the right answer most of the time. He did.

"Get your cute fanny out of that chair and come along with me," he said to Alicia.

She got up hesitantly, drawn features, bleached of color, eyes searching mine for some clue. "Tell him nothing, Alicia," I said. "We hold a pat hand."

I saw the little twitch at one corner of Cannova's mouth and I was ready for the blow, rolling with it. Still, his big flat cleaver of a hand knocked me off my chair to the deck. When I picked myself up, they were moving away. "Alicia!" I shouted, "Nothing. Not a word!" She turned bleakly, but he shoved her forward. They disappeared in the wheel house, the guard I later heard called Rick, remaining with me.

I could see them standing in the wheel house, Cannova resting one hand on her shoulder with false fatherliness, gesturing with the other, doing all the talking, Alicia shaking her head negatively. In a few minutes, Cannova seemed to grow vehement, then silent. I didn't like the silence. He stepped out of the wheel house and called something up to Halloran on the bridge, at the same time consulting his watch. Halloran put the stubby evil of submachine gun to his shoulder, cocked it and drew a tight bead on me. He stood relaxed and motionless. Even at that distance, the mouth of the barrel seemed enormous and gave the impression of looking between my eyes. There was the loathsome crawl of fear in my guts. I saw the guard, Rick, move back out of the line of fire. Then I had the sensation of steel wool rubbed along the nape of my neck.

In the wheel house, Cannova looked steadily at his watch, Alicia pacing, seemed to plead in the background. Then suddenly, she dashed up to Cannova and swung him around, speaking rapidly. For me it was one horrible pantomime. Then Cannova called up to Halloran and he slowly lowered the gun. I had been standing. I fell into my chair.

They came back down together and took seats as before. The *Barracuda* began to change course, almost reversing itself, but heading back obliquely.

Cannova was all smiles again. "It takes a little time," he said. "But there are always methods that work. For a minute there, I thought we were going to lose you, Keating. Just as I was getting to like you. But the little woman came through like a thoroughbred. Know where we're going now?"

"I could guess."

"We're going to park off the coast of Lauderdale. It won't take a half hour there and we'll be underway again. We'll take a boat through the surf and pick up the plates and the phony green. Won't take long at all."

I looked at Alicia. She hung her head.

"Come now, Keating," Cannova said. "You didn't expect her to let you die, did you? Of course, what she didn't know was that we would have let you die in sections, until she gave in. Oh well, let's talk of pleasanter things. Plenty of time for dying later. The delay is annoying, but on the other hand it's a beautiful day. I see all kinds of possibilities ahead and I feel truly magnanimous. Oh, one thing, Keating. Let's have the key to your apartment." He chuckled. "Breaking and entering is a serious offense."

It was useless. I gave him the key.

"I'll have one of the boys make us a highball." When we didn't answer, he signaled Rick and sent him below. He came back with the drinks on a tray. We took them and were damn grateful at that.

Cannova sipped thoughtfully a moment. He burped. "Ahaa," he said. "I have an extreme sense of well-being. And I feel talkative." I looked over my shoulder. Rick had resumed his place. Halloran watched with bored disinterest from the bridge. "I suppose, since you're not going anywhere, you have a certain curiosity about the past—and the future. The future can wait. I could spell it out for you in a sentence. Let's talk of the past. What would you like to know?"

Alicia and I looked at each other. I figured if we ever

came out of it, I'd like to have all the pieces. "Who was Emory and what was your connection with him?" I said.

"Emory was a big-time operator. He made and lost millions on the market. He was also a gambler at a time when I owned a night club with a den in back. He used to lose ten, fifteen thousand in a night. He cashed a lot of checks. Big ones. I had to O.K. them and I got to know him. We became friends of a sort. I told him I wanted to open a whole chain of places in Florida. He loaned me the money and became a silent partner. Then the market went sour, at least for him, and after awhile my clubs became his only source of income. When we were forced to close down, Emory was in a tight spot. And so was I. Meanwhile Emory had met McCabe at his brokerage office in Washington. They were very good friends. Emory introduced McCabe to gambling in Florida and later confessed he was running low on cash. McCabe told Emory he owned a set of the most perfect hundred-dollar plates in the world, plus a quantity of government paper and ink. He never would say how or where he got them. He needed a fast outlet for the money, the millions he was ready to produce. He knew that Emory had an interest in the clubs and he thought the money could be passed over the tables.

"He was only partly right. Some of the money could be passed over the tables, but we needed other outlets. Emory put the proposition up to me and I agreed to handle the distribution in the States, Europe and Cuba, providing the money was as good as McCabe said it was. McCabe turned out samples. They were so perfect we tested a couple on banks and had no trouble at all. So we agreed on a three-way cut with McCabe getting the largest percentage. McCabe went back to Washington and began stamping out the phonies.

"Meanwhile, I decided not to cut the take with anyone. I sent some men to Washington to snoop around McCabe and get their hands on the plates. McCabe spotted my boys, became suspicious and closed shop, hiding the plates. He trusted Emory, a softy with a peculiar code of ethics, and set up a deal with him to sell the plates for two hundred thousand in the event of his death, which even then was breathing down his neck."

"How did you find out about the deal George made with Emory?" Alicia asked in a shaky voice.

"I had become friendly with Millie. She told me."

"Did . . . did you kill my . . . my husband?"

"No. We had him prisoner here on the yacht. We weren't quite so watchful then. Before we could question him, he jumped overboard at night and drowned trying to make shore."

"God," Alicia said. "My God, how awful!"

"Why did you kill Emory, or have him killed?" I asked.

"He was killed against my orders by accident. He resisted when Halloran was taking him in for sweating. We thought he had the box at the time. He took awhile dying. He didn't know Alicia got away. And when we told him we'd kill her if he didn't tell us where the box was, he admitted it was at the airport. That's how we happened to be watching for someone to pick it up. Anything else?"

"What did you do with Emory's body?" I asked.

He sighed. "It's at the bottom of the ocean."

I knew then that we would be there soon ourselves. Or he wouldn't be telling us a thing. "How did you take Emory's place and why?" I wanted to know.

"That's simple. Millie, his wife, was about to get the boot. He was going to divorce her. I had sent Emory to Europe to close a deal for circulating the bills. I really wanted to get him out of the way. While he was gone, Millie was running around giving it to anyone who wanted it half as bad as she did and he found out about it. She sidled up to me and we worked out a deal. She didn't have any money of her own and I gave her two grand and promised her more. I moved in with her the day after Emory was killed. She fired the servants, then hired the Cuban girl. I knew it was just a question of time when Mrs. George McCabe here would come looking for Emory's widow. Where else could she go with the box? All I had to do was wait."

"Why couldn't Millie claim Emory's money since she was his wife?" I said.

Cannova laughed. "She didn't have a corpse and he hadn't trusted her with any joint bank accounts."

"Why didn't you just take the box away from us," said Alicia, getting back her courage. "Why did you have to offer to buy it at all?"

"Let's say it seemed easier to have you set it in my lap with the code and all than to risk any more killings or the danger of having you run to the police. I would have paid fifty thousand—that's all. Even I had to draw the line somewhere. And you were safe enough then because you didn't know what was in the box."

"But you found out that we did know, didn't you?" I said.

"Sure. Millie told us. With a little persuasion. I walked into her room unexpectedly and caught her listening to our conversation in the den. It was purely accidental. I had only come in to ask her a question. I heard Halloran's voice over her little radio. She sneaked out of the house but we caught up with her. Right, Keating? Anything else?"

"Where is she now, Cannova?" I said.

"Down below in one of the cabins. Would you like to see her? She's not very presentable, but . . ."

"She's dead, isn't she?" I said.

He smiled—almost sadly. "Very," he said.

"You dirty bastard."

"I didn't know you were fond of her, Keating, or . . ."

'You dirty, murdering bastard," I said.

"Be careful, Keating. We'll wash your mouth out with

salt water. And that brings me to your future. Or was there something else?"

I squeezed the chair arms to keep from hitting him. I did want to know one more thing, saturated as I was with the horror of knowing that Millie was dead below. "Were those plates stolen from the Bureau of Printing and Engraving by McCabe? Or did he make them?"

"That's one question I can't answer, Keating. I don't know. I don't think anyone in the world could make plates of their perfection. So draw your own conclusions. McCabe wouldn't tell out of some loyalty to the old man. Maybe the old man had something to do with it. But I doubt it."

"All right then, Cannova, what are you going to do with us?"

"We're going to drop you off somewhere between here and Cuba. That's where the equipment is."

"The equipment you stole from McCabe's workshop in Washington," I said.

"Right."

"What do you mean, drop us off between here and Cuba?" I knew perfectly well.

"Drop you off at the bottom, Keating. Your hash was cooked when Millie told us you knew about the plates. Nothing personal."

"And Alicia?"

He smiled wickedly. "I don't know about her. She'll certainly be last. You can just look at her and tell that, can't you, Keating?"

The first color crept into Alicia's face. "What do you mean?" I said.

"I mean that if she has to go, she'll have certain uses first."

My blood ran cold at his dirty leer, but, for the time being, at least, I was helpless.

CHAPTER EIGHTEEN

IT WAS TWENTY MINUTES past one in the afternoon. We lay anchored off the coast of Ft. Lauderdale, about a quarter mile from the beach. The sun had grown more intense. Our faces had the raw, baked feeling of being drawn tight with the heat and glare. The ocean remained calm. There was hardly a splash of surf in at the beach, the water alive with bathers bobbing at play.

It was an easy matter to lower the starboard launch, which, unlike its inboard-powered companion on the port side, was equipped with a Johnson outboard. I could see why they used the outboard. They were going to run it through the surf to the beach and the motor could be lifted from the stern so that the prop wouldn't churn itself into the sand.

Halloran went alone. At the last minute Cannova asked me where the true copy of the code was hidden. That was easy. It was with the plates. I told him.

The whole thing didn't take an hour. We watched Halloran follow the crest of a wave and gun up onto the beach. A small crowd gathered to watch and showed their enthusiasm by helping him pull the boat up out of reach of the water, then shove him off when he returned. The irony of it! It's almost funny the way people aid criminals unknowingly and with such cheerful energy.

Halloran came aboard smiling, the money and the plates in my small overnight case. While he was gone, the others were at least twice as watchful of us, prob-

ably because our chances of escape were so much greater if we ever got into the water. Alone I might have
made it, keeping under water for long intervals. But
there was Alicia.

We put out to sea again in high spirits. At least the
crew was in high spirits. Our morale was at its lowest
ebb when that shore began to fade.

We were left alone on the fantail until the horizon in
every direction held nothing but water and sky. Rick
had taken the wheel and the other one—Parlotta, I heard
him called—manned the rifle behind us on deck, Cannova
himself the submachine gun and Halloran, with him on
the bridge, the other rifle.

During the first hour after we left Lauderdale, we
kicked around various ideas and tossed them out one
after another as useless.

"Can't you think of anything?" Alicia said finally.

"I can think of a lot of things. But nothing anywhere
foolproof. And if we fail once, we'll never get another
chance."

"Don't you think," she said, "any attempt is better
than nothing? We don't have forever."

"I figure we have until nightfall. You may have a lot
longer. If we could jump overboard at night, we'd have
ten times better luck. It's not easy to find anyone in the
water in the dark. I say this—as soon as it's dark, if no
other opportunity shows, we jump in. I'll help you keep
afloat if you get tired. But remember, we'll have to duck
under water for long periods until we lose them. Think
you can do it?"

"I'll have to. I'll simply have to."

"All right then. When I yell "jump," don't hesitate.
Just go right over. Everything will depend on timing.
And luck. Stay right with me so we don't lose each other
in the dark."

"All that water at night," she said. "It makes me
shudder."

"Don't think about it. There are other things to make you shudder."

"Oh God, yes. Anything's better than . . . Any other possibilities?" She smiled weakly. "Like taking their guns—some kind of mutiny at sea?"

"Don't make me laugh. I've thought of all that. I might be able to slug one of those guys and take his gun. But I wouldn't risk it unless . . ."

"Unless what?"

"Unless I could get my hands on that machine gun. Whoever has the Thompson, controls the situation hands down. That's the key. I'd risk anything to get it. Give them a burst with that and it would be all over. But notice they don't keep it near us. It always dominates from the bridge. And I can't get up there."

"Maybe they'll come down with it later," she said.

"I'll be waiting for that. God! How I'll be waiting."

"And I'll be praying."

"Keep your wits and your courage, you'll need them."

"Burt. Oh, Burt. For God's sake, do something. Anything!"

"Cut it! Cut it right now. That's hysteria. We can't use it."

"Sorry."

"For your own sake. And remember . . ."

It sounded like a string of firecrackers thrown to the deck just beside us—or the sharp striking together of one of those New Year's Eve party clappers of wood, the sounds so rapid they fused into a single echo. We were hearing the fearful snap of the bullets, inches above our heads. The water just beyond us flew up thinly in a receding line shoreward. Alicia jumped half out of her chair, but I pushed her back again. I was just in time because another burst came right over our heads.

I looked around and above. Cannova held the smoking Thompson canted across his body so that the hot barrel didn't touch him. He jiggled with laughter. "Just testing!" he shouted. "Works fine. Dandy!" He passed the weapon to Halloran and came below. He approached us with a .45 stuck in his belt.

"I was getting bored again," he said. "How would you like to take a little tour? There's something I want to show you. Come on. Up!" He motioned us ahead of him, taking the .45 from his belt. Parlotta followed without being told.

We were shoved below, down a companionway, past a galley and half a dozen cabins. He paused dramatically at a closed door. "Thought you might like to say hello to Millie," he said. "Seems a nice thing to do under the circumstances." He watched our faces. I could see he was amusing himself with our reactions to horror. Alicia's face remained stony and I kept my own a mask. He looked a shade disappointed, but he opened the door.

She lay on the lower of a double bunk. Her face was a waxy white. Her dark hair was matted with blood and there was a blood smear on one cheek. Her eyes were open, immensely wide and empty. Her feet were invisible. They just disappeared—in a block of concrete!

On the deck below the bunk, there were two more of these blocks. They looked extremely heavy. It would take a strong man to lift one and carry it topside. Each block contained two foot-sized holes. Vaguely, I could see the shine of metal inside the holes.

Cannova saw how we stared at the block worn by Millie. "The latest style boot," he said. "What milady will wear at the bottom of the sea. Sometimes they call it the Mafia boot. Though we don't belong to the Mafia, we borrowed the idea. It's a modification of the cement overcoat. More portable and easier to handle. Would you like to know how it works?"

He walked over to one of the blocks on the deck. "When your feet are shoved into these holes, they rest inside the block in a rough, hollowed area. These intricate braces, made of stainless steel, are drawn about

your ankles so tight that sometimes the bones crack."
He chuckled. "Of course, by that time, you don't care
if your shoes are a little tight. You don't feel a thing.
The blocks are so heavy, you make a rapid descent to
the bottom, arriving feet first. And there you stand, waving, a kind of marine policeman, forever directing un-
dersea traffic." He smiled happily. "Notice that while
Millie wears one boot, there are still two more."

We stared at what used to be Millie with the ugly
fascination that death compels. I knew then that I
could kill Cannova, watch him die, and sleep like a baby.
I knew I would dislike myself afterwards only because
I had enjoyed it. Cannova began to speak again in the
manner of an intonation.

"There are places at the bottom of the ocean so deep
no man has reached them—no *living man*." He smiled
with mock sadness. "We think of being a hundred, two
hundred feet under water and unless we're professional
divers it frightens us. But those are depths for children.
Imagine resting on the bottom with a solid mile of water
overhead. The loneliness of it—the utter loneliness. And
the darkness. Not a ray of light ever filters through a
mile of water. Ever. In a thousand years. It's dark, it's
unspeakably lonely—and strange. Weird. Full of ugly,
writhing monsters, some never seen by man—slimy
things with only one basic urge—to gorge themselves
with food—any morsel of flesh that floats to the bottom.
They're not particular. They even eat each other. Marine
cannibals, a mile below the nearest breath of air. And
there are places where a mile would be considered
shallow water in comparison. Soon we'll be passing over
places of great depth—maybe not as deep as you could
find—but deep enough. It's a simple thing for us to
take soundings and find those deep, deep places.

"And think of the beauty of it from the standpoint of
one like myself who wants to conceal a crime—the cor-
pus delicti—without which there is no proof of murder.

They are always writing and talking of the perfect murder. It escapes me why so few have considered the perfection of the bottom of the ocean for hiding a corpse. Properly weighted, it will never rise to tell its silent story. And who in the world could or would search the tractless floor of the ocean, like searching a continent under thousands of fathoms of water. Marvelous! Don't you think?

"What's left of Emory stands under fifteen hundred feet of water. And who could find him? Not even I—if I wanted to. It's all very interesting. Tell you what, we'll let you see just how interesting when we lower Millie away."

"Tell me something, Cannova," I said. "Are you insane or just normally sadistic?"

"Oh, I'm not sadistic. Now you've hurt my feelings, Keating. I'm just interested in my subject. And my boys don't enjoy our mutual intellectuality. They're not as well read as we are. This is the first chance I've had to discuss the finer points, the more imaginative aspects of my crimes—as society would call them. I've enjoyed it.

"And now we'll take a look at the rest of the ship. Be my guests. After you."

We looked through half a dozen other cabins, all luxurious, some even equipped with their own bath. We had a glimpse of the big engines, the galley, finally pausing in a large lounge aft that served also as a chartroom and dining room. I never could figure why Cannova showed us around at all, except that he was insanely egotistical and the *Barracuda* was a matter of pride with him.

There was a bar in this room and while Parlotta held us under the gun, Cannova made us a drink. "A farewell drink," he called it. We drank it at the long table, in the center of which sat the steel box, empty of its treasure. Cannova held up his drink—"To the box," he said. "You can take it with you to the bottom as a little memento. We won't need it and it's a trifle dangerous to have around."

I kept staring at the box and the first shadow of a decent idea crossed my mind. Without appearing to do so, I studied the room. There were some enlarged and framed photographs of Cannova and his boys with assorted catches of fish. There was a large, open-mouthed barracuda, two dolphin and a sailfish mounted on the wall. There was also one of those CO_2 gas-operated spear guns hung on the wall, deadly, barbed spear protruding from the barrel. I had once been a skin diver of sorts and I knew that such a gun would fire its shaft through the tough, resisting hulk of a shark, or drive clean through a two-by-four. I would literally have given my right arm to have that gun in my hands, cocked to fire at the right moment.

Tilting my glass high, I also tilted my head so I could study the ceiling. I found what I was looking for—a hatch that opened onto the deck. I stored the whole picture in a careful corner of my mind.

We finished the drinks and were taken once more to the after deck where we were left alone with Parlotta covering us from his chair about ten feet away. Three feet to his right was the half open hatch to the lounge below.

Softly, I discussed my plan with Alicia. It all depended absolutely on timing. It depended mostly on a precise moment—the changing of the guard on the bridge. Now, Halloran held the machine gun. But there would come a time when Rick, at the wheel, would relieve him.

The time came at dusk. Rick climbed up to the bridge, munching a sandwich. Cannova was at the wheel. Halloran was getting ready to go below—I was sure to the galley for food.

I waited until Halloran and Rick faced each other, exchanging some commonplace preparatory to shifting the guard, in any case, not looking our way. And since we were aft and Cannova was at the wheel, his attention was ahead.

"Now," I said to Alicia. "It's almost dark. Now or never."

"Goodbye, sweetheart," she said. "Love and luck."

"Love and luck," I said.

She turned and walked toward Parlotta. I knew I couldn't get close to him on any pretext. She was only a woman—and beautiful. She could.

I watched. She spoke to him. He looked around her at me, saw that I was some distance away and apparently had nothing on my mind. He reached into his pocket and produced a pack of cigarettes. Up on the bridge, still not looking, Halloran was just handing over the submachine gun. I took that in and also the partly open hatch and Alicia's back hiding me from Parlotta at the same time.

On tip-toe, I moved quickly up behind Alicia. I gave her a gigantic shove. She was ready and unresisting. She fell mightily on top of Parlotta, tipping over his chair. Together they rolled on the deck. There was the small thump of their bodies, the clatter of the chair and Parlotta's rifle to the deck. There was wind and engine noise and distance. The sound had not carried to the bridge. Rick was inspecting the gun which Halloran had just handed him while Halloran looked on.

I threw the hatch cover back and jumped. I landed on the deck beside the table. I felt like my leg bones were being shoved up into my body. I crawled under the table as the pain and numbness subsided and came up standing on the other side. There was the muffled sound of shuffling feet on the deck and shouting. But no shot. Alicia was safe for the time, their whole concentration on me.

I reached up and removed the spear gun from the wall. I ran with it to the door, out of visibility from the hatch. I cocked the gun quickly and checked the spear to see if the line that ran from it was free. It was. The whole thing took seconds. I hid behind the open door—an idea just corny enough to work.

Heavy feet thumped down the companionway—the elephant sound of Cannova. I knew he would be first because he was closest. The upper half of Rick, rifle in hand, leaned down through the hatch. He didn't see me. He disappeared and I heard him running.

Cannova plowed into the room, the .45 in his big fist. I drew a steady bead on his barn-sized back but didn't like the shot. There was the sound of a half dozen feet scampering down the corridor, opening doors. It sounded like they hadn't even left a man at the wheel or one to guard Alicia. "Cannova," I called softly.

He turned and fired wildly in the same motion. I don't know where the bullet went. It didn't hit me. I was already squeezing the trigger when the shot came. There was the heavy woosh of compressed CO_2 released. Then there was a kind of sigh as the shaft fled from the gun.

It was something like those cowboy and Indian pictures you see with an arrow sticking in a man's chest—only ten times as shocking and real. The steel shaft caught him right below the Adam's apple and shoved on through his thick neck like it was paper, taking the heavy line with it. A thin stream of blood spurted half way across the room. He made a small gurgling sound and went over backward like a delinquent bowling pin.

There was no time to applaud. I grabbed the gun from his hand. It was cocked for the next shot. I hid behind the heavy oak bar, wondering why I hadn't thought of it in the first place. Rick was the first in the room. I recognized his voice. "Jesus, God," I heard him mutter. Then he shouted for the others. They came on the double.

I gave them just the moment it would take for them to crowd around the body—the moment before they would be running to the hunt again. Then I rose quietly but quickly. Their backs were to me. I knew they weren't going to obey any silly command like—Drop those guns, men!—while they had the Thompson or while there were three together. I decided to carry out my previous plan.

Using the bar to steady my arm, I drew a steady, perfect bead on the box. It was only a dozen feet away. I remembered not to jerk, but squeeze the trigger. I drew in a breath and held it.

They had seen me! I heard someone shout—"There's the sonofoabi . . ." He never finished it. But I finished the squeeze. At the same moment my wrist jerked with the recoil, on the leading edge of the sound wave, I flopped back behind the bar on my belly.

The two explosions followed each other so closely they collided—the box sound making a pigmy slap of the muzzle blast, overriding, drowning it. The room stood in suspension for an instant, then fell apart as though in the center of a thunderclap. There was nothing but sound. And then the heavy bar, torn from its mooring, tumbling down on my back.

I was losing consciousness even as I heard the brittle sound of lesser debris, wood splinters, glass, falling to the deck. I have no idea how long I was out. But it couldn't have been over a minute or two.

I opened my eyes and it was dark. There had been overhead lights before the explosion. I thought I was blind. Then I lifted my head. It struck the bar. I heaved. The bar fell away from me. My back ached like after three days of rowing. My ears rang like the echo of a bell that wouldn't quit. It was still dark. I peered upward.

Then I saw a small square of dirty grey light through the open hatch. The thought came to me that if the hatch hadn't been open the explosion might have blasted the sides of the cabin apart.

I felt in my pocket and found a lighter. I flicked it and it caught. The table was gone. There just wasn't any table. Only splinters on the deck. Glass, wood, fragments of stuffed fish and torn flesh were all over the room.

Halloran, who had been bending closest to the table, lay stretched across Rick, half his clothes and one leg blown away. Rick and Parlotta were just rag dolls, from which strawberry jam stuffing was oozing. The submachine gun, twisted shapeless, lay on top of the heap.

I saw this at a glance and without pity. The lighter was burning my fingers. I let it cool. Somewhere I heard the sound of water gushing. I relighted the lighter.

Sea water poured in from a jagged hole below the water line on the starboard side. It was slushing around my shoes when I stumbled through the debris and found the companionway. It was deep dusk on deck, but there was still light.

I found Alicia locked in the wheel house. I broke a window and got her out. "Don't talk now," I said. "We're safe if we hurry."

Someone had thought to cut the engines. We were drifting. Except for the ringing in my ears, it was immensely quiet. After Alicia was aboard, I lowered the launch on the port side, the one with the inboard motor. I climbed down a ladder and aboard. It took a minute or so to check the gas supply, start the motor, find the running lights and release us from the davit ropes. Then we gunned away. It was a very fast boat.

We circled the *Barracuda* slowly and from a safe distance, while I explained to Alicia what happened. In ten minutes the *Barracuda* developed a heavy list to port. Then she settled astern. In another five minutes the fantail disappeared beneath the water. The bow rose slowly to nearly perpendicular. Then with a sound not much greater than a sigh, she slid down, down, out of sight. The water closed around her, issued one gigantic bubble and the surface was as calm as before.

"I never thought I'd cry with joy when a ship went down," Alicia said with a hushed, awed little voice.

"It's lonely down there, Cannova," I said. "But you won't care. You won't care at all." And neither did I. Then I set a course by the dashboard compass and opened the throttle wide for shore.

CHAPTER NINTEEN

I DIDN'T KNOW where I was going. That is, I knew the direction of shore, but I didn't know the compass point that would take me to Miami. So when we saw lights along the coast, we pulled in about half a mile from shore and I tossed over the anchor. Huddled together, we fell into an exhausted sleep.

Dawn crept peacefully and beautifully into the sky. I awoke from a nightmare in which I relived the last hour on the *Barracuda*—a detailed horror picture without sound. Only the end was different. When the yacht sank, I was trapped in that cabin. The door was locked and I kept yanking on it frantically until the boat tilted at a crazy angle and suddenly the door was over my head. And then so was the water. I awakened gasping for air.

Alicia was asleep on my shoulder. I shook her gently. Her eyes grew wide, then enormous with fear. When she saw who I was and where she was, she began to cry softly. I stroked her head and let her finish. Then I said, "Were you dreaming, too?"

She nodded. "I dreamed that I stood at the bottom of the ocean. My feet were in cement blocks and I was under a mile of water. I was terribly tired and I wanted

to lie down. But on account of the blocks, I couldn't.
I couldn't lie down and I couldn't die. I was just going
to have to stand there, weaving with the current—forever.
It was so dark and I . . ."

"Never mind. Don't think about it."

"Don't think about it! I'll be dreaming it forever."

"No you won't. Maybe a few days, a week."

"But I'll never forget."

"Not entirely. But oh, how you'll appreciate life."

"Mere money, even two hundred thousand, won't be
important at all."

"Not for a couple of weeks or so. When I was lying in
a foxhole on Okinawa, I used to think if I ever got out
alive, I'd crawl in the gutter of any town or city is
America, sleep in a 'field, be a bum or a dishwasher and
be happy—never ask for another thing. I just wanted to
be alive in the States. But it doesn't last. In a month
you forget about the beautiful simplicity of just being
alive. Life becomes complicated with petty problems,
fowled up with installment loans, cluttered with things
and emotions, competitive drives, jealousies, incrimina-
tions and a thousand minor irritations. We forget."

"Let's not," she said. "Let's not ever."

"You sound like someone who has suddenly grown
up." I started the motor. "Come on," I said. "Let's not
tempt the gods any further. Let's see if we can find
Biscayne Bay and the terra firma of good old Miami."

It wasn't difficult to find anything in daylight. We
sped along the coast—then followed the causeway from
Miami Beach. This time we weren't jealous of the people
who waved at us from their cars.

We tied the launch in the same spot that had held
the *Barracuda*. Then we put the top down on the
convertible and let the morning air wash away some of
the filth of the night before—all the way back to Ft.
Lauderdale.

They hadn't fed us on the *Barracuda*. We were

having our first meal of the last twenty-four hours. Breakfast at Alicia's apartment. I couldn't get in my own place because my key was in Halloran's pocket at the bottom of the Atlantic. Later I told the manager I lost it and he gave me another.

After breakfast, really brunch, Alicia said, "I feel almost human again. What do we do now?"

"We should go and have a talk with the Miami police."

"Do we have to?" she said. "Right now? I've had all I can stand of this thing for a few hours. Why don't we take the rest of the day off and just lie on the beach?"

"Well, no one on the *Baracuda* is going any place, the plates and the phony bills went down with her, 'so I guess it can wait till morning."

"There's one bill that didn't go down," she said.

"Oh?"

She got her purse and opened it, removed the two halves of the torn hundred and handed them to me. "This and the launch are about all that's left of the whole dirty mess," she said.

"We ought to keep this as a souvenier," I said.

"Is it real?"

"I doubt it. But I don't think you'd have any trouble spending it if you got in a jam for dough."

"Let's each keep a half," she said.

"And then one day soon I'll present you with my half and we'll paste them together."

"What will that mean?" she said.

I studied her for a moment, thoughtfully. "It will mean," I said solemnly, "that two halves have joined together to become a whole."

"Do you mean what I think?" she said just as solemnly.

I nodded.

Her eyes moistened. She came over and put her arms around me. She kissed me carefully and tenderly. "Then we've got to hurry," she said.

"Hurry for what?"

"Hurry and get to know each other."

"You mean we don't know each other yet!"

"No. George always said you have to know each other under every circumstance. We've never played together. Like children. Come on! Let's start now. I'll change into my suit."

We lay next to each other on the beach. We looked out to sea and we were silent. It was a hard transition to make—from fear and horror to play. I wondered if, as Alicia said, we would ever again play like children.

The beach was crowded, noisy and gay. People chased each other into the water and down the beach as though there never had been, never would be trouble in the world. And I thought how we must look to them, lying there close together. Just two more in the carefree min of winter vacation fun. Certainly no one would believe that we had just now escaped from a lunatic nightmare of terror beyond their conception.

We did eventually talk of other things. Once we even laughed right out loud. We even went swimming. But in a way we were outsiders—and we were the only ones who knew it. So after awhile we got dressed and went out for cocktails and dinner. Then we came back to Alicia's apartment.

It was night. We sat on Alicia's patio and listened to the surf. We drank Manhattans and chatted easily. Some of the oppression was draining away.

During a lull in the conversation I had a quick picture of Bev. For once it was not the newspaper picture of her dangling from the wreck nor the pale wax of her at the morgue.

I remembered a small incident. We had in our bedroom, a battered alarm clock. Once it had fallen to the floor and the plastic case had broken. But the clock still worked. It was a time of economy and we decided against buying a new one. Then one day it didn't go off and we were late for work. The next morning it rang as ever. We talked idly of buying a new one, but we never did.

A couple of weeks later, on Valentine's Day, we both came home with our little packages. When we opened them, each contained a shiny new electric alarm.

It was a strange, funny-sad little thing, the unity of thought that comes in marriage. But I remembered now the grin spreading over her face, the way she laughed as we sat at the dining room table comparing the two clocks and trying to decide who had made the best choice. That was Beverly. And this was Alicia. And I felt close to each in a different way.

"I was just thinking of Bev," I said. "A funny little experience we had together."

"Tell me," she said.

I told her.

"When you can remember things like that instead of . . . well, anyway, you're out of the woods," she said.

"I know. That's what I wanted to say. I'll always love her in a special way. But the morbid part is gone."

"It just goes to show . . ." Alicia began, but then the phone rang—sharply and repeatedly in the other room. Her head turned to me in the moonlight. I saw her eyes widen. She gripped the arms of her chair.

"Relax," I said. "And answer the phone."

She got up hesitantly and toying nervously with her hair, walked on egg shells into the other room. The phone stopped ringing. There was a short conversation I couldn't hear. She came back smiling and sat down with a deep sigh.

"I never thought," she said, "that a wrong number would be so welcome." Then we both laughed—a little hysterically, but with vast relief.

I never felt so close to anyone as I did at that moment —even Bev. I had a sudden impulse. I took something from my billfold and handed it to her.

"What's this?" she said. "Why—why it's the other half of the hundred! I thought we said that . . ."

"I just happened to think—they might want it for evidence tomorrow. Besides, I wouldn't have been able to hold out more than a day or two."

She got out her half and like excited children, we ran into the living room to paste them together.